Two For The Price Of One

Montana Cowboys 3

Sandy Sullivan

EROTIC ROMANCE

Secret Cravings Publishing

www.secretcravingspublishing.com

Sandy Sullivan

Secret Cravings Publishing Book

Erotic Romance

TWO FOR THE PRICE OF ONE (MONTANA COWBOYS 3)
Copyright © 2011 by Sandy Sullivan
Print ISBN: 978-1-61885-142-0

First E-book Publication: October 2011
First Print Publication: December 2011

Cover design by Beth Walker
Edited by April L'Orange
Proofread by Belinda Barton
All cover art and logo copyright © 2011 by Secret Cravings Publishing

ALL RIGHTS RESERVED: This literary work may not be reproduced or transmitted in any form or by any means, including electronic or photographic reproduction, in whole or in part, without express written permission.

All characters and events in this book are fictitious. Any resemblance to actual persons living or dead is strictly coincidental.

PUBLISHER

Secret Cravings Publishing

www.secretcravingspublishing.com

Dedication

This addition to the Montana Cowboys series is dedicated to my mother, Catherine Mauch. She was my biggest fan and read every one of my books. She told me once if she would have been 30 years younger, she would have been all hot and bothered after she read one of them. I lost her unexpectedly in May of this year at the age of 81.

Thanks for being there and believing in me, Mom. May God keep you by his side until we see each other again someday.

TWO FOR THE PRICE
OF ONE

Montana Cowboys 3

Sandy Sullivan

Copyright © 2011

Chapter One

Emma Weston tapped her fingers on the steering wheel of her old truck and sang along to the song on her radio. Singing wasn't her thing, but she loved many of the country bands, their songs and the singers. Man, did she love the singers. The gorgeous guy hanging on her wall at home, Brandon Tucker, was her favorite. She'd give about anything to meet him. Every wet dream she'd ever had centered on his gorgeous body.

Her cell phone interrupted her daydreams of said hunk—Brandon Tucker's voice sang "The Love of My Life," which happened to be her absolute favorite, as the call from Becky came in.

She hit the talk button on the phone sitting in the plastic cup holder attached to her dashboard and asked, "Hey, Bec. What's up?"

"You're going to the rodeo this weekend, right?"

"Yeah," she said, glancing in her rearview mirror out of habit. Her dad constantly scolded her about being aware of her surroundings. You never knew when a stray cow, horse, goat, or some other farm animal might wander into the road. Life in rural Montana came with all kinds of accidents involving animals. "I'm ridin' remember?"

"I forgot. You know how scattered brained I am sometimes," Becky answered.

Emma laughed. "I know, but I love you anyway, Bec." She and Becky had been best friends since kindergarten. "Are you working the beer stand with me?"

"Yeah. Seth asked me to fill in."

"I don't know why you two don't just start datin' and get it over with. You've been moonin' over each other for a year now."

"I can't, Em, you know that. He's too old for me. My daddy would have a cow."

"He's only a few years older than you," she said, giving Becky the same speech she'd already given her over and over regarding the very sexy Seth Reardon who owned the local honky-tonk. "We're both in our mid-twenties, and Seth is in his early thirties."

"It seems kind of weird though."

"Oh, I don't think it is at all. Just don't think of him being older. I mean, look at me. If I could rope Brandon Tucker, I'd be there in a heartbeat, and he's five years older than me."

"Not even a comparison, Em. He's gorgeous, rich, hot, and one of the biggest country music stars to hit the stage in years. He may even be bigger than George."

"No one is bigger than George, but Brandon has it all goin' on. I mean, if I could have ten minutes— Holy fuck!"

The screech of tires as Emma yanked on the steering wheel of her truck and slammed on the brakes echoed along the lonely stretch of highway between her parents' place and town. The crunch of metal and the hiss of her radiator when the fluid inside gushed from the cracked engine rang in her ears as she shook her head and peered out the windshield.

"Emma? Emma, talk to me." Becky's almost hysterical voice came out of the plastic container, now on the floorboard.

"I'm okay, Becky. Do me a favor though and call the police, and have them come out to… Shit. I'm not even sure what intersection I'm at."

"They'll find you. Don't worry. I'll call right now. You were on your way to town from your parents', right?"

"Yeah."

"Hang tight. They'll be there soon."

"Thanks, Bec," Emma replied, listening while the phone disconnected when Becky hung up.

Emma hit the snap on her seat belt to unhook it and then pulled the handle on her door while she pushed against it, trying to get herself out of the truck. It groaned and creaked like a little old man's bones when he tried to stand up, but it finally opened, and she crawled out.

Shielding her eyes from the glare of the Montana sun in the middle of August, she saw the front end of a massive brown and black bus with fancy scrolling on the side smashed into the front of her pickup. "Crap. Dad will kill me for this."

"Are you all right?"

Emma turned around quickly only to have spots form in front of her eyes and her head begin to spin.

"Whoa. Easy there, darlin'."

The deep, rich, smooth as silk voice and the feel of strong hands cupping her elbow to hold her steady had her looking up into a set of dark brown eyes framed by the longest eyelashes she'd ever seen. Only one person she knew had those pretty eyes, and he graced the wall of her bedroom. Collar-length dark hair, windblown by the rustling prairie gusts, wide chest with mouthwatering muscles straining his black T-shirt, trim hips holding up the low-riding jeans, and dusty cowboy boots—holy shit!

"Brandon Tucker?"

"Never mind who I am, honey. You're bleedin' from the cut on your head," the man replied, pulling a handkerchief from his back pocket and pressing it to her forehead. "Hold this on there a minute. It'll help stop the blood."

"What the hell is goin' on here?" an angry voice said from several feet away. "Damn it, Beau."

"Beau?" she asked, totally confused as the second man came storming in their direction from near the door of the bus.

Wait a damn minute here. There are two of them? No way! Two Brandon Tuckers?

"Sorry, darlin'," the first man replied before pushing her down on the bumper of her truck. "Stay there a minute while I deal with him." He walked back toward the agitated man and said, "Knock it off, Brandon. It was an accident. I didn't see the stop sign."

The two men moved toward the front of the vehicles, but Emma could still hear the angry voices.

"An accident? Fuck! Look at the front of the bus. Shit, shit, shit. This is gonna take days to fix, and we're out in the middle of bumfuck Montana, Beau. How do you suppose we're going to get this fixed in time for me to be in South Dakota next week, huh? I have a show to do."

"I realize that, Brandon. Stop acting like the spoiled star and listen to me for a minute. There's nothin' we can do about it right at the moment. They're gonna have to tow both of these into town, and we'll deal with it after we talk to a mechanic."

"We don't have a body shop big enough to handle a bus, but we aren't far from Billings. You could possibly have them tow it there," she said as she stopped next to them and held out her hand. "I'm Emma Weston, and if I'm not mistaken, one of you is Brandon Tucker. Care to explain to me why there are two of you? Or am I seeing double because of the crack in my skull."

"Brandon, quit being a jerk. She's hurt for cryin' out loud," Beau snapped and then turned back toward her. "Sorry, honey. You really should be sittin' down or somethin'. Concussions can really suck. I know. I've had a few."

"Thanks, but I'm fine. Now, explain why there are two of you."

"It's not common knowledge, but yes, there are two of us. We're twins," Beau replied, running his hand through his dark hair.

"Identical?"

"Well, duh." The smart remark came from Brandon as he leaned against the bus and crossed his arms over his chest.

She glared at him and then turned her attention back to the first guy.

"I'm Beau, and you're correct. He's Brandon Tucker."

"*The* Brandon Tucker?"

"Well, d..." Brandon started, but snapped his mouth shut when Beau glared.

"It's nice to meet you, Emma. I wish it had been under better circumstances," Beau said, taking her hand between his. "How's your head?"

Emma could hear the distant blare of police sirens getting closer, telling her several cop cars or at least one car and an ambulance were close. "It hurts, but it'll be fine." She glanced over her shoulder as one of the police cars skidded to a stop, followed by two more. *Damn. The entire Red Rock police force is out here. All three of them.* "I'll take your handkerchief home and wash it for you. It's got blood all over it."

The police officer jumped out of his car and slid to a halt at her side. "Emma? Are you all right?"

Great. I do not *need the overprotective, whinny Alex right now.* "I'm fine, Alex. Just a bump on the head."

"I'm calling an ambulance. You need to get checked out at the doctor."

"No. I don't want to go to the hospital."

"Your daddy will have my hide if you don't get checked out, Emma. I'd rather keep it, if you know what I mean."

"I'll deal with my dad, Alex."

"What happened, anyway?" Alex asked, shoving his sunglass up on top of his head.

Emma tried not to giggle at the sight, but with Alex's premature balding, the sunglasses made him look like a beetle with his eyes on top of his head. He really was a nice guy, and he'd had a crush on her since high school. Unfortunately, she couldn't even think of him in any sort of a romantic way. He would always be Alex the tuba player from band.

She glanced again at the two gorgeous hunks standing nearby with their hands in the pockets of their rugged jeans and T-shirts molded to identical sculpted chests. Never in her life had she thought she'd have a chance to meet Brandon Tucker, and here she stood with two of them. *Two? How come I've never heard of him having an identical twin brother? I know everything about Brandon Tucker, from the size of his shoes to the brand of underwear he wears.*

Beau caught her gaze with his, and the sexy little twitch of his lips as a small smile spread across his face made her blush and go hot all over. Blood rushed to her head, and she felt woozy again, but this time she wasn't sure if it was from the bump or the hot look from Beau.

Next, she took in his brother. *The* Brandon Tucker. The one man who tantalized her dreams at night with wet kisses, hot licks, and the oh-so-gorgeous body. So far, Brandon's attitude left something to be desired. He definitely acted like the spoiled music artist as she listened to him talk to the police officer taking his statement.

"I really think this whole accident is her fault, officer. She couldn't have been paying much attention if she missed a vehicle the size of this bus. I mean, she ran right into us."

"Excuse me?" she said, moving closer when she heard his words. "You ran the stop sign. I don't have a stop sign on my side of the road, buster."

"She's right, Brandon."

"Shut up, Beau. Let me handle this."

"Don't you tell him to shut up, you overbearing, think you know it all, spoiled pain in the ass. Just because you're a country music star doesn't mean shit out here. I live in this town, and your money and your fame aren't going to get you anywhere." Indignation raced through her blood at Brandon's high-handed attitude.

Beau's lips twitched as he stepped back to watch. Emma wasn't sure how she felt about him letting her do all the standing up to his brother, but right now, she didn't care.

"Listen here," the officer said, but backed off when Emma got right in Brandon's face.

The CD player in her truck started playing, for no apparent reason, and what else came on? Brandon's newest CD.

"A fan?" Brandon mocked, one eyebrow cocked arrogantly over his left eye as he stood nose-to-nose with her.

"Not anymore," she snarled and then walked to the side of her truck. With the window down, she crawled inside, popped the disc from the player, and walked back to Brandon's side. "See this?"

"Yeah," he growled.

The cocky grin on his face disappeared when she snapped the disc in half, pulled her arm back, and flung the pieces into the nearest wheat field.

* * * *

Emma Weston had him, Beau Tucker, tied up in knots the moment she crawled out of her wrecked truck. Her soft, singsong voice wrapped itself around his nuts and squeezed, reminding him exactly how long it had been since he'd found a woman worth fucking—not some buckle bunny and not some music groupie, but a real, honest-to-goodness woman.

When she'd come out of nowhere and he'd hit her truck with his brother's bus, he'd been scared to death someone in the vehicle might be badly hurt. Thank goodness she wasn't. The wound on her head might need a stitch or two, but she was walking, talking, and cussing with the best of them. Standing at probably five foot six or so, she would fit right nicely against his six foot frame. Her willowy body, long brown hair, and big blue eyes left him wondering exactly what she'd look like in nothing but a sexy thong.

"Fan or not, Brandon Tucker, you're a jerk," she snapped and then turned on her heel to walked toward Beau. "I'm sorry, Beau. Is he always like that?"

He shrugged and said, "It depends. I'm used to it, I guess." A quick glance at his brother revealed his narrowed eyes resting on Emma. "I think he had a bit too much to drink last night after the show we did in Idaho. He's probably hung over."

"Hung over or not, it's no excuse for being rude."

Hoping he'd have a chance to get to know Emma better, and knowing Brandon would be a part of anything they started, he said, "Give him a chance, Emma. He's really a nice guy most of the time."

"Hmrph."

A short laugh burst from his lips when Emma made the little pouty sound and folded her arms. "You're cute when you pout."

"I'm not pouting."

Before he could stop himself, he smoothed his thumb over her bottom lip and said, "Yes, you are."

Her pretty blue eyes dilated, and her breathing sped up, making her tempting breasts rise and fall with each breath. By her reaction to his touch, he could almost believe she felt the attraction between them too, and for once he realized it wasn't Brandon she wanted this time. Whenever he met a woman he had to wonder if she actually wanted him, or if it was because he looked just like his brother, the infamous Brandon Tucker. With his brother's attitude sometimes, you would think Brandon was the older of the two of them by ten minutes and not him.

Unfortunately for him, Brandon got the voice and Beau got shit. Well he shouldn't say that, really, since he also got the rugged good-looks, dark brown eyes, nice smile, and hard body like his brother. Except Beau turned out to be the nice guy, and Brandon had turned into the spoiled star as women threw themselves at him, begging for attention. Brandon used them and tossed them away like yesterday's garbage most of the time. His brother's behavior bothered Beau. Women meant more to him than a passing one night stand, even if he hadn't found the one girl he wanted to spend the rest of his life with.

Born and raised on a ranch in eastern Montana, they both knew the meaning of hard work, long days, and pushing horns. From an early age, Brandon stood out amongst the crowd. He'd started singing at rodeos, fairs, competitions, and anywhere else he could find an audience. Beau'd tagged along with his brother, managing Brandon's money and his career, and keeping him out of fistfights with jealous boyfriends. Today, he'd had been behind the wheel of the bus due to their driver's having a family emergency back home.

"I'm real sorry about the accident, Emma," he murmured, wishing he could pull her in closer and feel her lips under his.

"It's okay," she whispered, her breathing shallow and her face flushed with what he hoped might be excitement and curiosity. Her tongue came out to lick her lips, catching the pad of his thumb in the process and sending white hot need straight to his dick.

The rough clearing of a throat brought his attention back from where he'd been drowning in Emma's eyes.

"I've called the tow truck, Emma," Alex said, stopping next to them.

Beau wanted to hurt Alex for interrupting the charged moment between him and Emma. The need and desire swimming in Emma's gaze fascinated him.

"Thanks, Alex," she replied, breaking contact with Beau and stepping back. "Can I use your phone so I can call my dad?"

"Here. Use mine, Emma," Beau said, pulling the phone from his pocket. "It's the least I can do."

"Thanks. I'd use mine, but it's buried on the floor of my truck somewhere. I was talking to Becky when the accident happened."

"You were on your phone?" Alex asked, narrowing his eyes. "You know it's illegal to be on your phone."

"I had her on speaker, Alex, so it wasn't illegal. I wasn't texting or anything. I don't do that."

"I'll have to put it in my report though."

Her eyes narrowed, and Beau hid his smile. "Well, make sure you qualify it with all the facts."

"I will, but you know your insurance company might have problems with it."

"It wasn't my fault, Alex. Beau admitted he didn't see the stop sign."

"Here," Beau said, showing her how to operate his phone with a touch to the screen. "Now you can dial regular."

"Thanks again," she said before she moved away.

Several moments later, he could hear her trying to explain to someone on the other end.

"No, I'm fine, Dad. There isn't any need for you to come out here. They'll be towing the truck into town in a few minutes. The tow truck just got here."

A lapse in conversation made him wonder what her father said on the other end, but Beau's attention drifted away the moment her eyes met his. *Pull your head out, man. She's just another babe—and I hope to hell she's nowhere near jailbait, but with women these days, a guy has to be careful.*

Beau shook his head and walked over to the tow truck driver to see about getting the bus towed into town or somewhere they could get it looked at. Brandon had abandoned the party for the inside of the bus the moment the police officer finished with his statement, leaving Beau to deal with everything. *Figures.*

"So. Are you going to be able to tow the bus, too?" Beau asked the driver as he hooked up Emma's truck.

"Nope." The man wasn't forthcoming with information, and he continually glanced Emma's way.

"Do you know Emma?" Beau asked when he saw the man look at her again.

That got the driver's attention. "Yeah. Known her since she was a little girl. Why? You know her?"

Beau shrugged and said, "Only since I hit her truck."

"You were drivin'?"

"Yes. How bad are the damages to hers?"

The man squinted and then spit a string of tobacco juice at the ground, almost hitting the tip of Beau's boot. "Bad enough her daddy's gonna have a few words for ya. The drive train's probably busted, and the radiator and engine are cracked, if I had my guess, by the fluid on the ground under it. I'd say several thousand dollars in damage. You're just damned lucky she ain't hurt. You don't want to mess with the Weston bunch. I'm kinda surprised her brother Cade ain't out here yet." They both looked behind the bus as a large diesel pickup came screeching to a halt on the road behind them. "Spoke too soon."

"Emma Leanne Weston!" the man driving the truck shouted the moment he cleared the door.

"Aw shit," Emma said, walking back toward Beau. "Here's your phone back. Thanks." She turned back around and met the guy halfway. "Chill, Cade. I'm fine." The man wrapped her in a hug and then stepped back.

"Are you sure you're okay?"

"It's just a bump on the head. I suppose Daddy sent you out here."

"Of course. I was on my way back to my place when he called me on my cell." The man she called Cade glanced over her shoulder and locked his gaze on Beau before he glanced back down at his sister, frowning. "What the hell did you do, Emma? You couldn't hit somethin' smaller like a stop sign. You had to hit a bus?"

Beau took the moment to approach the pair, noticing the similarities in their coloring. They shared the same hair color and penetrating blue eyes. "Hi. Um, listen. It wasn't her fault. I ran the sign. I just didn't see it."

Cade looked at him and then back at Emma. "He looks awful familiar. Isn't he the guy you have plastered all over the walls of your bedroom?"

The look on Emma's face almost had Beau laughing. Color bloomed on her cheeks and spread down her neck. Surely there weren't that many shades of red.

"Actually, no, I wouldn't be the guy. Name's Beau Tucker," he said, holding out his hand. "The guy on her wall is probably my brother Brandon. We're twins. He's the singer. I'm the bus driver. At least today I am."

Shoulders back and eyes narrowed, Cade gave Beau the once over and then pushed his hat back on his head and held out his hand. "Nice to meet you, Beau. I'm Cade Weston, Emma's older brother."

"Did you have to embarrass me, Cade? Jesus. I have one damn poster," she snapped throwing up her hands. "You can tell Gabrielle and Dad I'm fine, and I'll be home after they finishing towing the truck in."

"No can do, sis. If I go back there without you, I'll never hear the end of it. I won't even be able to hide at my house, because Nat will harp on me about it too."

"God, I love my sister-in-law," Emma said with a chuckle.

The cell phone in Cade's pocket rang. "Excuse me a sec." He opened it and held it to his ear. "Yeah, I know. I've already told her."

The murmurs on the other end of the conversation sounded like an irritated mother to Beau. He knew all about them, since he dealt with his own parents. Whenever Brandon's face got plastered all over the tabloids about this escapade or that, Beau got to explain it and make excuses for his twin's reckless behavior. Their folks didn't seem to understand Brandon was a big boy and could take care of himself.

"Well, there is a bus involved, Dad." Cade rolled his eyes. "No, not a school bus or anything like that. It's actually a musician's tour bus." A few more murmurs and he said, "All right. I'll ask, but I can't make any promises. They might be busy or on their way somewhere. Bye, Dad."

"Don't tell me," Emma grumbled.

"You know Gabrielle, Em," Cade replied and turned toward Beau. "My Dad is requesting your presence at the home place for dinner. It's the least we can do, since you've been inconvenienced by this whole thing."

Excitement zipped down Beau's back and settled in his balls. He could actually spend a little more time with Emma if he and Brandon took the invitation. Brandon would kill him, but right now, he didn't care. "I accept on behalf of myself and my brother. We'd love to have dinner with your family. Plus, it would give me a chance to apologize to your father about getting his daughter into an accident."

Emma glanced at him and frowned, although her eyes blazed with heat. Maybe he read her wrong. Maybe she wasn't attracted to him like he thought. He cocked an eyebrow and then glanced down at her chest. Nope, no mistaking the tips of her nipples poking out. Lucky for him, his dick had calmed down a little since he'd stood so close to her, but if she didn't stop looking at him like she wanted to eat him alive, it wouldn't take long for it to rear its head and point right at her.

"Can I talk to you a second?" she asked, taking his arm and pulling him along until they stopped several feet away from the crowd.

"Is there somethin' wrong, darlin'?"

"Listen, you don't have to come out to my dad's place. He likes to get all friendly and stuff."

"But I'd like to."

"Why?" she asked, putting both hands on her hips.

"I'd like to spend a little more time with you. You know, get to know you a little better. I know we didn't meet under the best circumstances, but maybe fate stepped in."

She stepped back and put her hand up to her throat. "I...You...Really?"

"Yeah, really. I'd like to find out what makes you tick. What better place than at your family's house?"

The door to the bus opened, and Beau rolled his eyes. *Great. Just what I need—Brandon out here again.*

"Beau, can I talk to you a minute?"

"Stay right here, Emma. I'll be right back."

They moved several feet away, and he could tell Brandon was gonna blow. He'd probably heard Cade issue the invitation even from inside the bus, since they'd had the side windows open while they drove.

"I'm *not* going to anyone's house for dinner, Beau. I want to find a decent hotel in this shithole town, drink until I'm numb, and then pass out."

"You mean like you do every night?"

"What's it you? You get paid to keep everything straight."

"Maybe I'm tired of being your pansy, Brandon, and digging your ass out of a jam every time we stop somewhere and you get an itch for some pretty thing in the front row. Personally, I don't care whether you go out to Emma's dad's place or not. I'm going, once we get the bus settled. It's getting too late to be doing anything this evening anyway, and it would be a nice reminder of home, having dinner with an ordinary family. I bet they'd even treat you like you were normal, Brandon, and not some high class musician."

He pushed past Brandon, but stopped a few feet away and turned back to face his brother when it dawned on him why Brandon didn't want to go out there. "I get it. This whole not wanting to go out there is because Emma isn't fawning over you and kissing your ass. In fact, she's so pissed at the way you've been acting, she broke one of your CD's and tossed it into the field over there. It's got your goat that you just lost a fan, and you don't know how to handle it, much less the fact she's gorgeous. You're attracted to her too, aren't you? We're usually attracted to the same type of woman, and I bet this is no different."

Brandon rushed to his side and hissed, "All right, fine. She's hot. Okay? And I don't like her drooling all over you and not me. I'm the star here, and it should be me she's gettin' all hot and bothered over, not you. I saw the way she got all gooey when you brushed your thumb over her lip."

"You know what, Brandon? You're an ass and a jerk, just like she said. Maybe she likes nice guys instead of assholes. I aim to find out, whether you come along or not. But let me warn you, if you do go out there with me for dinner, you better take a step or two back and remember how our parents raised us. Lose the megastar attitude and at least pretend to be a nice guy for a change." Without waiting for a reply from his open-mouthed brother, he walked back to Emma and Cade and said, "Why don't you give me the address, and once we get the bus settled, I'll take a cab out there."

"Is Brandon coming?" Emma asked, and Beau wondered why.

"I don't know."

"Yes, I'm coming, and thank you for the invitation," Brandon replied, walking back to where they stood near the back of the bus. "And I promise to behave," Brandon replied with a smile.

Emma scowled, and one dark eyebrow shot up. Her apparent irritation with Brandon made Beau feel much better. Maybe he wouldn't have to compete against his brother for a woman's affection this time. Maybe Emma didn't really want Brandon after all.

"It's settled then. We'll catch a cab and—" Beau said.

"Nonsense," Cade replied. "I'll take everyone into town, and then once everything is settled, we can all ride out to my parents' place together. I'll call Nat and have her meet us there with Alan."

"Beau, why don't you ride with the tow truck driver now that the bigger rig is here to take the bus into town? I'll ride in with Cade and Emma," Brandon said with a satisfied smirk.

Beau wanted to punch him. "But I—"

"You need to handle all the details, brother. You know more about those kinds of issues than I do. Of course, we'll be right behind you, right Cade?"

The arrogant asshole attitude Brandon wore like a suit jacket, shined brightly for all to see as Brandon shoved Beau out of the way and situated himself in close contact with the beautiful Emma.

"Uh, yeah," Cade said with a frown and a strange look as he ushered Emma towards his truck.

"Don't, Brandon."

"What?" Brandon asked, with a wide-eyed innocent look Beau didn't believe for a second.

"Just don't, or I'll kick your ass," Beau snarled. He spun on his heel and headed for the front of the bus.

Chapter Two

Emma watched, openmouthed, as Brandon charmed every one of her sisters during dinner. If she didn't know better, she would have sworn Brandon and Beau had switched personalities in the time it took for them to get the bus situated, and for Cade to drive them all back to the home place.

From the moment they'd stepped into the house, Beau had snarled and snapped, while Brandon smiled and suckered every female in the house into loving him. In another words, he turned into the Brandon Tucker Emma fantasized about with every breath she'd taken since he'd burst onto the country music scene some five years before.

With a shake of her head, she pulled open the sliding glass door between the living room and the back yard and stepped out into the night's cooler air. Orange streaks painted the evening sky while the sun fought gallantly against the coming darkness. She loved Montana evenings in the summer. They always seemed so romantic—given you were spending them with the right person. For Emma, the right person had yet to come along, but she couldn't wait to find him.

Outside lights flicked on as the sun disappeared, bathing the backyard in a soft blue glow. Tonight's full moon and the clear night sky would make an awesome backdrop for a couple of lovers. "Yeah, right," she murmured.

"Emma?"

She spun around to find one of Tucker brothers headed in her direction. From this distance, she couldn't tell whether Brandon or Beau had stepped outside. Earlier, she'd noticed they both wore distinctive and different colognes, making it easy for her to know who was who if they were standing close enough, since she didn't know them very well…yet.

"Brandon. What are you doing out here?" She tipped her chin up and folded her arms over her chest. "I'm sure the other women of my family will miss your company."

"Will you mind if I go back inside?" he asked, stepping close enough to touch.

The warmth of his breath on her face made her shiver, and she didn't like her reaction at all. "What do you care?"

"I care. You're a very beautiful woman, Emma." One finger skimmed down her cheek and then slipped along her jaw.

With a sharp jerk, she pulled her face away from his touch. "Don't play games with me, Brandon. I'm not fooled by your change in personalities. You were a total jerk at the accident."

"I know, and I wanted to apologize to you. I don't usually act so arrogant."

She didn't believe him for a second and the small snort she released told him so. His earlier behavior screamed arrogance and righteousness.

"I see you don't believe me."

"I didn't say that."

"You didn't have to. I could see it in your eyes."

Her body went into overload when he stepped close again. Goosebumps rose on her arms, and a shiver raced down her spine as the spice of his cologne wrapped around her senses and the warmth of his skin called to her.

"You have beautiful eyes. They remind me of a crystal clear lake." His fingers slipped down her cheek in a soft caress. "I wonder—do they go dark like sapphires when you're aroused beyond rational thought?"

His voice trailed off into a whisper, and his mouth came close enough that if she leaned in, she could feel the firmness of his lips and find out if her fantasy Brandon was anything like the real thing. Did she dare? He'd be gone in a heartbeat when the bus got fixed, but what if she let herself pretend he could fall in love with her? What about Beau?

"Your lips look so soft, Emma. I need to taste you."

Her eyes slowly closed as he nibbled at the corners of her lips and then trailed kisses back toward her ear. His teeth nipped at the soft skin of her neck, sending her thoughts scattering to the wind.

The moment his mouth brushed hers, she couldn't think—couldn't breathe. Everything revolved around his lips and his oh-so-wicked tongue as it pushed into her mouth, demanding she give in to her desire. Without thought her arms went up around his neck, and she returned his kiss lick for lick, nip for nip, and sigh for sigh. Brandon the fantasy and Brandon the real man merged into one. She could no more resist him than she could go without breathing.

The feel of his hand skimming up under her shirt and then cupping her breast drove a whimper from deep inside her to the surface of her lips. The calluses on his fingers from playing the guitar were rough and exhilarating at the same time. A soft mewl escaped her mouth when he lifted his head.

"That's it, darlin'. Give in. You know you want me," he murmured as his lips trailed down her neck.

"Can't do it, can you Brandon?"

Beau's voice, coming from her right, slammed into her like a cold rain—bitter and freezing. Desire cleared like a fog bank cut by the early sun, and she stepped back out of Brandon's arms to face a very angry Beau.

"Beau, listen—" she started, but he cut her off.

"Don't, Emma. It's fine. I'm sorry I read more into the attraction I felt for you. I thought you might have really liked me for me, and not because I'm Brandon Tucker's twin."

Irritated beyond belief, she tried again to make him listen. "No, Beau, you don't understand. Let me explain."

"I do. Really. We go through this a lot, don't we Brandon?" he asked his brother, while Brandon just shrugged and examined the fingernails of his left hand.

"You what?" she snapped. Anger filled her when she realized the whole thing was a game between them. See who could get the girl to give up her panties the quickest. "This is like a game to you two. Is that it? I'm some kind of a fuckin' conquest?"

"Emma, listen," Beau said, stepping closer with his hand outstretched, but she backed away.

"No, you listen. Get out! Both of you. I don't fuckin' care how you get back to town, and I don't want to see either of you ever—and I do mean ever—again." She took two steps toward the door, but Beau grabbed her arm and spun her around. With her temper in full flare, she balled up her fist and connected with Beau's jaw, dropping him to the ground. "*Don't* touch me," she snarled.

Just as she reached the door to the house, Cade came outside and said, "Everythin' okay?"

"No, it's not okay. I want those two out of our house."

"What happened, Emma?"

"Nothin'. Leave me alone. Just get them out of here." Before she could stop them, tears streaked down her cheeks. How could they do this to her? Megastars didn't care about anyone but themselves, and apparently twin brothers didn't either. The lifestyle of a country star must have rubbed off on Beau too.

The moment she reached her bedroom, she threw herself across the comforter on her bed and sobbed. She'd really thought Beau might have been different, and when Brandon had actually started acting like a normal human being, she thought she'd been wrong about him too.

"Emma?"

"I don't want company," Emma mumbled into the blanket.

She felt a warm hand on her hair and the mattress sinking under her as Natalie sat down next to her.

"Honey, I'm sorry things turned out this way."

Wiping the tears from her cheeks, she whispered, "It doesn't matter, Nat. Neither of them are worth the tears."

"So why are you crying so hard?"

"Because I actually was stupid enough to think they might have been different."

"They?"

She turned her head and looked up at her sister-in-law. "Can I ask you a question?"

"Sure, honey."

After a fortifying breath, she asked, "How did things go down with Cade and Kale? I know you dated both of them for a bit."

Natalie bit her lip and slid into the chair next to the bed. "I'm not sure if you really should hear about it." The worried expression on Natalie's face gave Emma pause. Maybe she shouldn't pry. After all, Natalie was married to her brother, and Kale had found his own love with Laurel. "Will you answer a question for me first?"

"Sure."

"Are you thinking you like both of them?"

Emma sat up on the bed, looked up into the gorgeous face of Brandon Tucker on her wall, and sighed as she wiped the tears from her cheeks. "Yeah. It's wrong though. I shouldn't be attracted to both of them."

"Why not? It's kind of hard not to be when they are identical twins."

With a shrug of her shoulders, she said, "But Beau is completely different, or at least I thought he was. He seemed so nice when he helped me out at the accident. Brandon was such a jerk out there, but when he got here, he turned into the guy I always fantasized about—sweet, charming, and hot enough to melt butter."

"You want to tell me what happened outside?"

"Brandon kissed me."

"And?"

"I totally lost myself in him, Nat. I didn't hear anything around me. Nothing penetrated the blood rushing in my ears, except when Beau came outside. The way Beau sounded…" She shook her head. "I felt dirty and used."

"Why?"

"They made it out to be like some kind of competition between them. Who could get in the girl's panties first or somethin'."

"Mmm."

"So please, tell me what happened between you, Cade, and Kale."

Natalie took one of her hands and said, "I came out here to help my gram after grandpa died. I know you've heard about how I ended up in a ditch, and Cade came to my rescue."

"Yeah."

"Well, apparently he told Kale about how he'd run into me, so Kale came over to see for himself. I ended up having lunch with Kale and dinner with Cade."

"Wow," Emma whispered. "You have to tell me. I've heard rumors, you know, around town, but I didn't want to pry."

"The rumors I had sex with both of them?" Natalie asked, pink staining her cheeks as she looked down at her hands for a moment.

"Um…yeah. But it wasn't like at the same time or anything, right?" she asked, totally in awe that someone sweet and grounded like Natalie would date two such different men.

When Natalie lifted her gaze, Emma could see the sparkle in her eyes at the mention of having sex with the two men. "It's true, and yes, it was at the same time."

Shocked and dismayed to find out the rumors she'd heard were true, Emma asked, "Seriously?"

"It wasn't planned or anything, Emma. Cade and I had a huge fight earlier in the day. I was desperate to make your brother pay for his big mouth. The attraction

I felt for Kale wasn't anything like I felt for Cade, but saying I was pissed would be an understatement. Your brother had insisted he didn't care if I dated them both, or even had sex with them both."

"He actually said that?"

"Yes. Anyway, I told Kale I wanted to have sex with him, and he agreed. He told me he'd pick me up. Well, when he showed up, both he and Cade were there. They pretty much kidnapped me and took me out to Kale's place. The thought of having both of them together intrigued me, so I asked them if they would, since they'd shared before, and they agreed."

"How was it?"

"Intense, but afterwards I realized I loved Cade, and what had happened wouldn't happen again. Now Kale is happily married to Laurel and has a great family with Kimmy and their new baby, Cody."

"It's not uncomfortable around Kale?"

"No. We're all best friends, including Laurel."

"Does she know about what happened?"

"Yes, and it's something we just don't discuss. It's in our past, and it's not like we ever planned to make it a permanent threesome."

Emma's gaze searched out the poster again. Brandon's kisses outside had turned her inside out, but she wondered if Beau's would do the same thing. The feelings Beau had aroused when they stood so close together out by the bus said yes, but without actually kissing him, she'd never know. Certainly the desire the two of them created in her seemed far more intense than anything she'd ever felt before with any other man.

"I can see those wheels turning, Emma. What are you thinking?"

"I'm not sure. I know how Brandon's kiss affected me, but I haven't kissed Beau."

"You could get burned badly if you're thinking what I think you are."

"I know," she whispered. "And I truly wish I wasn't contemplating having sex with both of them. It's a once in a lifetime opportunity. I hate to think they're competing for me like two little boys fightin' over a toy. If we do this as a threesome, I think it would take the competition thing right out of the equation."

* * * *

The hotel room door banged against the wall as Beau stormed inside and Brandon followed closed behind.

"Fuck!" Beau snarled, tossing his bag onto the couch.

"Easy, Beau," Brandon said, hoping his brother wasn't going to do something stupid like put a hole in the wall.

"Screw you, Brandon. You aren't the one standing here with a goddamn golf ball-sized bruise on your jaw."

"She packs quite a punch." He threw his suitcase on one of the beds and reclined back against the headboard. Emma Weston intrigued him. She didn't fit into the mold of fangirl and she didn't bow to his charms or throw herself at his feet begging for his attention. The attraction definitely sizzled between them. No doubt there, but she wasn't sure what to do with it. He knew what he wanted to do. A quick fling would be right up his alley. But Beau wanted her too.

Maybe he should step aside and let Beau have a chance at her? Be the kind a caring brother for a change.

"How did I let you screw this up so bad?"

"Listen, Beau. I'm sorry. Okay? I did instigate the kiss, but I wasn't prepared for the effect of it when she laid it on me."

"Wasn't prepared? How can you not be prepared, Brandon?" Beau threw up his hands and paced like a caged lion. "You've got girls fawning all over you, throwing their bras up on stage, half stripping next to the bus to get a piece of you and all you can say is, 'I wasn't prepared'?"

"Emma threw me for a loop, Beau. She's not like the other women I run into." He rubbed his chin. Women usually came along easy—too easy most of the time, if he were honest with himself—but Emma made him *feel*. His heart raced, and his palms felt clammy when she stood near. And when he'd kissed her? Oh hell! His brain had refused to function and his body had gone into overload, shunting all the blood to his dick in an instant. At first it seemed to be the normal reaction he had around a gorgeous woman, but the longer the kiss went on, the harder it was to think beyond the feel of her lips under his and how perfectly her breast fit into his hand. He shook his head to free himself from the fog of desire and said, "How many fans of mine do you know would tell me off like she did, break my CD, and toss it into the field?"

"Not many," Beau agreed, his features still stone cold. "But I should never have made it sound like we were competing for her."

"We usually do."

"And you usually end up with them," Beau grumbled. "But she's different—special."

"Neither of us knows her at all, Beau. How can you say she's special?" Brandon had never heard Beau talk like this about a woman, and it had him a little worried. Yeah, it would be great to get a little piece while they were stuck in Montana, but falling for a woman wasn't in his plans. He needed Beau with him, and if his brother got tied up in knots over a female, it could certainly through a wrench into their immediate future.

Beau grabbed a beer from the six-pack they'd bought at the local market, popped the top, and slumped into the chair by the window. "I wish I knew." Beau opened his mouth to take a swallow and glared at Brandon. "Damn this hurts. I'm gonna need some ice on it pretty soon, or I won't be able to open my mouth at all tomorrow."

"So what are we gonna do to get back into Miss Emma's good graces, huh?" Brandon asked, lacing his fingers over his stomach.

"We?"

"She wants us both, Beau."

Beau frowned and took another swallow. "How would you know?"

"I kissed her, remember?"

"Don't remind me, asshole."

Brandon sat up on the side of the bed and dangled his hands between his knees as he glanced over at his brother. "You're just sore because I got to her first, but I have a feelin' you'll get your chance."

"Oh yeah?"

"Yeah. I think she's confused. I mean come on, Beau. We've shared a woman or two—"

"One or two or twenty."

Brandon grinned and shrugged at the small smile on Beau's lips. It didn't matter how many they'd shared in the past, he wanted to share Emma. "She responded to me, but she did to you too—out by the bus. I saw the way she melted under your touch."

"Yeah, but I didn't have my lips all over her and my hand on her tit," Beau snapped.

"I didn't mean for it to go that far so fast. It just happened, but I'm not gonna apologize for it, because it was damn nice. Fit perfectly in my palm."

"Fuck, Brandon. Stop already. I'm gettin' hard thinkin' about her," Beau replied, adjusting his cock in his jeans.

"Makes two of us then."

"So what are we gonna do about it?"

"Hell, I don't know." He grabbed a beer and popped it open. "We could always kidnap her. You know, take her on the road for a couple of weeks."

Beau looked at him like he'd lost his mind, and yeah, he probably had. "You aren't serious, are you?"

"No, I guess not, but it's a thought. I mean, she used to be a fan. She'd probably have a great time on the road."

"Oh yeah. Watching how many women throw themselves at us. Goin' from place to place, barely stoppin' to eat." Beau took another healthy drink. "Somehow I don't think she'd be too thrilled."

"But that's our life, Beau, and I won't apologize for it."

"It doesn't mean she'd like it."

Beau frowned, and Brandon started to worry. He knew Beau was getting tired of the road life. They'd talked a lot about settling down, buying some property and finding a good woman, but neither one had found anyone he wanted to settle down with. "What are you thinkin', Beau?"

His brother downed the rest of his beer and stared at the can, twisting it into a mashed mess of aluminum. "I don't know, Brandon. I'm gettin' tired of this life, but we always agreed I'd be there for you, no matter what happened or how long it took for you to reach your dreams."

Brandon took several sips of his beer, contemplating what life had given him. From early on, he'd been able to sing. He'd always been told the baritone of his voice gave women goose bumps, and he'd played on it, using it to get any woman he wanted. After he broke into country music, he'd lived the high life. Money and fame brought things he'd only dreamed of as a kid.

Their parents weren't rich by any means, but they did all right, and with what he pulled in now, he tried to take care of them for a change by having Beau send them money. He glanced at Beau and shook his head. He couldn't imagine being in this life without his twin next to him. Lately, he'd started thinking about what Beau had given up to be with him on the road all the time. Beau hadn't mentioned his dreams recently, and maybe it was time for Brandon to ask. Red Rock seemed to be a town where they might be able to sit for a few weeks and relax. If Emma Weston came into the picture while they were here, then so much the better.

"What about your dreams, Beau?"

"I don't have any." Beau jumped to his feet, tossed the can in the trash, and began to pace.

Brandon watched as Beau paced from the door to the bathroom and back. "Sure you do. I know you do. You wanted to get some land and raise cattle, like Mom and Dad. Find you a pretty woman, settle down and have a passel of kids."

"One problem, brother. There isn't a pretty woman who wants to settle down with me anywhere around here and we aren't done with your career yet."

Silence stretched between them for several moments, but their thoughts were so in tune, they didn't have to speak to understand each other, or at least for each to have some idea of what the other thought. Brandon knew he surprised his brother when he said, "You know what? I think we need to take a break."

"A break?"

"Yeah. The bus is down for at least two weeks according to the mechanic here in town. Let's cancel the four shows we've got coming up. We can reschedule them. I know we planned on stopping by Mom and Dad's on our way through, but I think it's important for us to stay here."

"And do what?" Beau asked, clearly puzzled by Brandon's wish to spend some time in Red Rock.

"Stay here. Find out more about this little town. There's a woman worth pursing right here, and we both want her."

"You've sure changed your tune from this morning, when you called it a town in the middle of bumfuck Montana." Beau's eyes narrowed, like he wasn't sure if Brandon was serious or not. "What if she doesn't want us?"

Not want us? Is he serious? "Are you crazy?" he asked, wondering if his brother had really gone over the edge. The challenge of one Emma Weston called to his blood, and he knew Beau felt it too.

"She may be attracted to both of us, Brandon, but do you seriously think she'd be interested in dating us both to decide if she might want one of us?"

Brandon let a sly smile lift the corners of his mouth before he said, "Who says she has to choose?"

Chapter Three

Emma glanced across the street to check for oncoming traffic and then made a beeline from one side of Main Street to the other as she headed for the diner. Her plan today included lunch with Becky and then heading out to the rodeo grounds to get things set up for the weekend. She knew exactly where the two guys taking up a lot of her thoughts were staying, and she wanted to get the work she'd volunteered to do out at the rodeo done so she could focus the rest of her evening on them.

"Emma Weston."

Shit. "Uh, hi Laurel."

"You know better than to cut across the street," Laurel said, from where she leaned against her patrol car. Laurel wasn't tall for a woman at five and a half feet tall, but she had the muscles to back up her police work. Her red hair and dark blue eyes caught the attention of several men in town, but her temper was all redhead when she got pissed off.

"Sorry, Officer. Won't happen again." Unfortunately, her innocent act wouldn't work on Laurel. She'd been around Red Rock too long to be fooled by it. Laurel had moved to town a few years earlier to help her sister with an abusive husband and ended up married to Cade's best friend, Kale. Laurel was usually cool, but very bossy when it came to police stuff.

"Uh-huh," Laurel replied with a cheeky grin. "Where are you off to so fast?"

"Lunch at the diner with Becky before we head out to the fairgrounds. Are you on patrol all day?"

"Yeah." Laurel lifted her sunglasses from her eyes and gave Emma a once-over.

"What?"

"You're wearing that?"

Emma looked down, taking in the white tank top molded to her breasts, the skinny jeans showing off the soft swell of her butt, and the cowboy boots made of the softest leather available on her feet. "What's wrong with my outfit?"

"Plan on ropin' you a man, girl?"

She couldn't stop the little smile on her lips. "Maybe. One or two."

"Two, huh? Sounds like the story I got from Elizabeth might have some merit to it."

"What story? I'm gonna kick her ass for her. I don't care if she is my sister, she needs to butt out."

"Whoa, honey. I'm sure she didn't mean anything by it," Laurel said, placing her hand on Emma's shoulder and squeezing lightly. "She's worried about you."

"There's nothin' to be worried about." She pulled her shoulders back and stuck out her chin with a stubborn tilt. "I'm only out for a little fun while two of the most gorgeous men I know are in town. Once they leave, it'll be back to another small town Saturday night."

The look Laurel gave her said Laurel really didn't believe a word Emma said, but would stand by her, no matter what happened in the end. "Just don't lose your heart, Emma."

"In a few days? Ain't gonna happen, Laurel."

"You comin', Emma?" Becky yelled from the diner doorway.

"Be right there." She turned back toward Laurel and gave her a hug. "Thanks for the advice, but everythin' will be fine. I don't have any intention of losin' anythin' to Brandon or Beau Tucker other than a few hours of my time."

"I hope you're right. Be careful, huh?"

"Always. Catch ya later, Officer." She kissed Laurel on the cheek and turned toward the diner. A moment later, she slid into a booth across from Becky. "Wow, it's warm out there today."

"It sure is. I'm already sweatin' down between my boobs, and I ain't even gotten started yet."

The two of them shared everything—boyfriends, periods, dates, sex and men. Not necessarily in that order. Emma knew she could tell Becky anything, and she usually did—but right now the embarrassment of being attracted to both men made her feel like she needed to keep Brandon and Beau a secret.

"What happened with your accident the other day? I heard you hit a bus."

"I didn't hit them, they hit me, but yeah, it wasn't pretty. Screwed up my truck pretty bad."

"Whose fault?"

The waitress returned with their drinks, and Emma took a sip before she answered. "The driver of the bus. He didn't see the stop sign."

"Wow."

"I'm glad I wasn't hurt, and no one on the bus was, either."

"I saw the bus at the garage earlier today."

Crap.

"Why didn't you tell me the bus belonged to Brandon Tucker, Emma? I thought we shared everything. And then I find out from your sister, for goodness' sake, that you had him at your house last night for dinner."

"Well, I..."

"Hey, Emma."

Holy hell! Emma didn't even have to look to see who stood at the edge of the booth. If Becky's round eyes and slack jaw hadn't told her, the tingle down Emma's arm from his touch would have.

"Brandon." She looked behind her, spotting the bruise on his jaw, and stammered, "S–sorry, Beau. I thought..." *Damn it. They aren't wearing cologne today.*

"It's okay, darlin'. Happens all the time." The smile on his face made her leery. She'd been so pissed at the two of them the night before, she didn't understand how she could look at him now and only think about finding out if Beau's kiss would do the same thing to her that Brandon's did.

She bit her lip and dropped her gaze to the middle of his chest. The blue T-shirt stretched across the expanse of muscle and the jeans riding low on his hips had blood rushing in her ears and liquid gushing from her pussy.

"Wait! There are two of them?" Becky said, her voice almost a squeal.

"Mind if we join you?" Brandon asked, walking up behind Beau.

"Sure. Of course," Becky replied, before Emma could say a word.

Beau sat down beside her and Brandon slid into the booth next to Becky, who sat there with her mouth open.

"Becky, close," she told her, indicating with her hand that Becky should shut her mouth.

"But it's Brandon Tucker and..." She looked at Beau. "And Brandon Tucker."

"Becky, this is Beau Tucker. He and Brandon are twins," she replied, indicating the pair. "Guys, this is my best friend, Becky."

"Nice to meet you, Becky," Beau said, holding out his hand.

Becky took it and blushed to the roots of her red hair when Beau brought it to his lips and kissed the back of her hand. The green-eyed monster of jealousy reared its ugly head, and Emma had to fight it down with a swift mental talking to. Unfortunately, it got twice as bad when Brandon did the same thing.

Emma cleared her throat and said, "What are you two doing here this time of day? Don't you, like, stay up all night and sleep all day?"

"We do normally stay up pretty late, but we had to talk to the mechanic at the garage this morning," Beau replied.

"When did they say the bus would be fixed?" she asked. "I know you've got shows to do the next couple of weeks."

"Oh yeah. Total fangirl over there," Becky said, ignoring the glare she shot her way. "She knows every stop you have on your schedule between now and Christmas."

"I'm flattered," Brandon replied, giving Emma a dimpled grin.

Emma completely forgot to think, breathe, or swallow. *If these two turn on the major charm, I'm so totally screwed.*

The waitress came back to their table to take their order, and both men made themselves at home, ordering lunch and drinks while they kept up the conversation with Becky.

Emma felt lost. Yeah, she'd planned to flirt and make sure they knew she'd forgiven them for what happened last night, simply because she had plans to use them a little herself. Why not? Two gorgeous men seemed interested in her, and even if they would only be around for a few days, she planned to use and abuse them just like they'd planned to do to her. She hadn't planned on jealousy rearing its ugly head when they flirted with Becky.

After their food arrived, Beau asked, "So what are you two beautiful ladies up to this afternoon?"

"We have to help set up tables and stuff at the beer tent for the rodeo tomorrow."

"There's going to be a rodeo this weekend?" Beau asked, giving his brother a strange look that Emma couldn't quite decipher. Brandon shrugged and shook his head slightly.

"Yeah. It's a huge deal here. Founder's Day and all, but they're donating all the proceeds of this year's rodeo," Becky answered.

"To what?" Brandon asked, stuffing a french-fry in his mouth.

"There's a local family who has some really crazy hospital bills to pay. Their daughter has a brain tumor and needs treatment, but they don't have the money to have it done right now. We're raising money for them," Emma said.

Brandon and Beau looked at each other, and then Brandon pushed his plate away.

"Aren't you hungry?" she asked.

"Not really. I…um. I'm full."

Emma didn't think it had anything to do with his being full. The sadness in his eyes made her wonder what kind of tragedy these two shared.

She shrugged and kept talking. "Anyway, all the proceeds from admission and the sales at the beer tent are for them. Everyone thinks there will be a huge crowd."

"Who owns the beer tent?"

"A guy named Seth Reardon. He owns the honky-tonk up on the corner of Fifth and Onion."

"Onion?" The chuckle coming from Beau's mouth focused Emma's attention on his full, oh-so-kissable lips, and she had the insane urge to lean over and lock her lips on his.

She cleared her throat instead. "Yeah, Onion Street. They didn't get real creative when they named some of our streets."

Brandon stood and looked toward the counter for a moment. "Listen, we'll catch you girls later, okay? I have an errand I need to run, but give Beau the directions out to the fairground, Emma, and we'll help you and Becky set up."

"Seriously?" she asked, not sure if he was joking or what. "Brandon Tucker, mega country star, help us set up chairs and tables?"

"Yes, seriously. I'm no stranger to hard work. I had to set up band equipment plenty of times before I had a road crew." Brandon signaled the waitress for the check and handed her a hundred dollar bill. "Keep the change, honey."

Beau got to his feet and then leaned over to tuck a piece of hair behind Emma's ear. The whole world narrowed to his face, his eyes, and his smile. "We'll see you in a bit, darlin'." He leaned over and brushed his lips against hers lightly, leaving her mouth tingling, her nipples taut, and her pussy screaming for attention.

"Hello? Emma?" Becky waved a hand in front of her eyes, bringing Emma back from her fog enough to realize the two guys had left.

"Huh, what?"

"I lost you there for a minute—or should I say several? The second he kissed you, everything disappeared for you."

"Damn. Am I that obvious?"

"Uh, yeah. Duh. You've been half in love with Brandon Tucker from the moment you laid eyes on him. And now? To have a twin brother too? How in the hell will you ever choose?"

"Who says I plan to choose?" she asked, with a cheeky grin and wicked thoughts running through her mind.

* * * *

An hour later, Emma and Becky arrived at the fairgrounds and headed for the beer tent. Seth already had guys moving in and out with cartloads of kegs, barrels, and plywood for the temporary bar, along with plastic chairs and a few tables so people could sit and mingle. The makeshift Boots and Spurs would be open for business when the sun went down. The rodeo didn't start tonight, but one of the local bands always played, giving everyone a chance to unwind after the long work week, sip some beers, and visit with friends.

Emma glanced toward the back of the tent and caught Seth giving Becky a look hot enough to set the tent ablaze while Becky set up tables and chairs near the front of the tent. Those two were so attracted to each other, the room popped with the electrical current they gave off, but both seemed too damned stubborn to break the barrier they'd erected between them. *Maybe I'll play matchmaker a little tonight.*

"Hey, Seth," she said, moving close to where he stood.

Seth Reardon could set a few hearts to skipping with his rugged good looks, hard body, and striking green eyes. He was homegrown Montana boy to the core. Born and raised right there in Red Rock, he'd had several girls all over him in high school, but he was very shy around women. Clumsy and awkward in school, he'd quickly earned a reputation as a geek. Shortly after graduation, he'd gotten contacts, worked out at the local gym, and beefed himself up. When his daddy had died several years ago, he'd inherited the local honky-tonk, and ran it with an iron fist—but he never seemed to find the right girl.

"Hi, Emma. How are you?" he replied, never taking his gaze off Becky.

"I'm fine, but Becky isn't."

"What's wrong with Becky? She isn't sick is she?" The look of concern in his eyes told Emma he cared for her friend…a lot.

"Yeah."

"Well, she needs to go on home then and get some rest. Being out here in this heat probably isn't helping. I'll tell her right now."

"Easy, Seth. She's not sick as in nauseated or whatever. She's heartsick."

"Heartsick. What the hell is that? Some new thing?"

"Since you came along, yeah."

"You're confusing me, Emma. Either she's sick or she's not. Which is it?" Seth tapped his food impatiently and folded his arms across his chest.

"Are you completely blind, Seth Reardon?" she asked, throwing her arms up and scowling.

"I have no idea what you're talking about, Emma."

"The two of you are half in love with each other, but all you do is give each other scorching looks across the room."

"I've tried, Emma. She won't go out with me. She says we can't be anything but friends."

"And do you know why she thinks that?"

"No," he replied, tapping another keg and avoiding Emma's gaze.

"She thinks you're too old for her."

His eyes narrowed, and he snorted softly. "I am not. We aren't more than a few years apart."

"Five, to be exact, but who's counting?" Emma shrugged her shoulders and laid a hand on his arm. "You need to convince her age doesn't mean anything. You two are perfect for each other, but if you don't speak up, she's gonna find someone else."

The sinfully smooth voice of Brandon—or was it Beau?—interrupted her conversation. "No flirtin' with the boss, darlin'."

She spun around and came face to face with both Tucker men. *Damn it. These two are too luscious for my sanity.*

"Hey you two. Have you met Seth?"

"Uh…yeah. Sort of," Beau replied. "Nice to see you again."

"Sort of?"

"We met him earlier, Emma, when we went by the bar to talk to him," Brandon added.

"It's great of you to do this, Brandon. It's going to be phenomenal. I already have someone working on flyers and stuff, since we don't have a lot of time to get the word out," Seth said, wiping his hands on a towel. "We already have a makeshift stage the band tonight will use. If you have a couple of amplifiers, we'll be all set.

"I've already let my fan club president know so she can spread the word too. Fans are great for letting each other in on what's goin' on. I wish we had the whole band, but acoustic will have to do."

"Okay, wait a minute. What are you two talkin' about?" she asked, totally confused as her gaze went from Seth to Brandon and then to Beau.

Beau took her hand and brought it to his lips. "Brandon is gonna do an acoustic show here tomorrow in the beer tent to raise money for the little girl's family you told us about earlier."

"Really? That's like… Wow," she whispered. Her heart swelled with awe for these two men who'd blown into her life like a tornado, bowling her over and twisting her up until she didn't know who she was anymore. "Whose idea was this?"

"Brandon's initially, but Seth jumped on it when we talked to him at the bar," Beau replied. "We've spent the last couple of hours getting things together and trying to let everyone know."

Overwhelmed with gratitude, she hugged Beau and then Brandon. "This is amazing. I can't believe you're doing this for someone you don't even know."

Brandon said, "I could tell it was important to you by the way you talked about it at the diner. It's the least I can do, and it's not a big deal, really."

"Yes, it is Brandon. You have no idea how much this will mean to them. And Charlene is a fan of yours, so it will be so much sweeter for her."

"Cool. Then she should have front row seats," Beau said.

"Along with my number one fan," Brandon added, brushing his lips against her cheek. "If you're still my fan."

"It's gonna take a little more convincing, I'm thinkin'," she whispered in his ear then bit the lobe. "But you're on the right track."

"Okay, enough of all this. We've got work to do," Becky shouted from the corner of the tent. "I thought you two came here to work?"

"Yeah, yeah," Beau replied. "Show me where the pack mules are gatherin' and I'll put my back into it." He slapped his brother on the shoulder, pulled him out of Emma's embrace, and pushed him off toward the group of men moving equipment, but not before he glanced over his shoulder and gave her a playful wink.

Fighting the urge to sigh, she leaned against the beer keg and licked her lips.

"If that isn't the look of a woman wantin' a couple of hunky men, I don't know what is." Becky said, walking up beside her.

"Yeah, well. It takes more than just wantin' to get some, Becky."

"Don't I know it," Becky replied, pulling out a chair and sitting down as she watched Seth moving around behind the bar.

Emma pulled out a chair and sat next to her. "You know, I talked to Seth a bit before Beau and Brandon came in, and he wants to take you out."

"I know."

"You know? How come you won't go out with him, then?"

"I told you, Emma. He's too old for me."

"I've never heard anything so crazy in my life."

"You don't understand. I dream of him all the time. Hell, I go to sleep at night thinking about him after I've used my vibrator. I'd give anything to have his hands on me." Becky sighed and placed her elbow on the table. "Why the hell do you think I help him out when he asks me to? It isn't for the money."

"Then what's stopping you, Becky?" she asked, and then waved her hand in dismissal when Becky started to object. "Besides the age thing, because that's just an excuse and you know it." Emma watched her friend pick at a crack on the table without looking her in the eyes. "You can tell me, Becky. We've been friends forever, and you know I'll never judge you."

When Becky lifted her gaze, Emma saw tears swimming in her eyes. "He's Jewish, Emma. My father raised me Baptist, and he'd never, ever let me date a man not of the Baptist faith."

"But…but you aren't really even a practicing Baptist."

"I know, but my father would never give me his blessing to date a man outside of our faith. You know how old fashioned he is."

"God, Bec. I wish I knew what to say." Emma's heart bled for her friend. Although she'd never been in love, she couldn't imagine not having the blessing of her father, her brothers, and her sisters when she did find the man she wanted to spend the rest of her life with.

"There's nothing to say, Emma. I'll never know the feel of his hands on my skin, the taste of his kiss, or how it would feel to have him make love to me. I can't go against my father. He would disown me, and if things didn't work out with Seth, I would have no one."

"You'd have me and my family. You know that. None of us would turn our backs on you."

"Thank you," she whispered, squeezing Emma's hand. "We need to get back to work. There are still lots of chairs and things to get set up before the crowd shows up later."

Without another word between them, they walked back outside to grab more chairs, but Emma couldn't quite get her friend's dilemma out of her mind. There had to be a way to help Seth and Becky get together, and she needed to figure out how.

She'd grabbed one of the huge empty trash cans and took it around behind the tent to start picking up the mountain of miscellaneous garbage from the bar set up when she was grabbed around the waist and hauled up against a rock-hard chest.

Chapter Four

Scared out of her mind, Emma elbowed the hard body behind her and reared her head back, smashing the man in the nose.

"Fuck!"

She quickly spun around at the sound of the man's voice and dropped to her knees beside him. "Oh my God! Beau, I'm so sorry. You scared the hell out of me. Are you all right?"

"Hell no, woman! You probably broke my nose to go along with the damn bruise I still have on my jaw." He tipped his head back as bright red blood dripped from his nostril and pinched the bridge of his nose. "A guy needs to be careful around you, or he could get hurt."

"Wait right here, I'll get some napkins." Cussing under her breath, she rushed into the tent, grabbed a handful of paper napkins from the table, and ran back outside. "I'm sorry, Beau, really. I didn't mean—"

"Its fine, Emma. I know I startled you, but damn, woman," he said, his speech garbled by the paper.

"Here. Let me see." She removed the wad under his nose, but he still continued to bleed. "I'm gonna to get some ice for you to put on the bridge of your nose. It'll stop the bleedin' better."

When she rushed back inside the tent, Brandon asked what the fuss was all about. She reassured him everything would be fine before she ran back out again with the ice in a towel. Beau had moved to a picnic table nearby and leaned back against the edge.

"Lay this on there," she said, placing the ice on his face and then leaning over to kiss the spot she'd bruised earlier. "I guess I should stay away from you. It seems all I do is hurt you."

"Not on your life. I'll take my chances if it means holding you, Emma. Just warn a guy, would ya?"

"Well, you shouldn't have grabbed me."

"Yeah, I kind of gathered you don't like bein' startled."

"Cade taught me how to defend myself. You got to be my test dummy."

"Great. Now I'm a dummy." Beau sat up with a small grin on his lips, wiped the remaining blood from his face, and set the ice down on the table. "I think it's quit."

Unable to stop herself, she brushed her lips against his for a moment, tasting what she'd been dying to since the moment she laid eyes on him.

The moment she lifted her head, he said, "I think I might need another one. You know, for medicinal purposes."

Grinning like the cat that ate the canary, she scooted closer and pressed her mouth over his. The moment their lips touched, her body caught fire from the tips of her toes to the roots of her hair. A soft moan broke the stillness of the evening, but she didn't quite know if it came from him or from her. Her arms went up around his neck, and she tilted her head as his tongue dove between her lips to slide along hers. How could two men look so much alike but kiss so differently and taste so good? Beau's hands did a slow crawl down her spine and then cupped her hips.

Moments later, she found herself straddling his hips, kissing him like the sun wouldn't come up in the morning if she didn't give in to these feelings he stirred.

Warmth covered her back and a second set of lips found the edge of her earlobe, sending her desire skyrocketing out of control. Teeth nipped, and a tongue played along the skin of her neck while she continued to kiss Beau. Having two men touching, licking, nipping, and focusing solely on her desire had her groaning in frustration the moment Beau's mouth released hers.

"Don't stop."

"We can't continue this out here, honey. Too many eyes," Brandon whispered in her ear.

The evening air sent shivers down her back when Brandon stepped back and helped her scoot from Beau's lap. When she glanced down, there was no mistaking the bulge in his jeans.

"You do this to me, darlin'. You drive me nuts," he growled, taking her hand and pressing it to his cock.

Startled by the fierceness in his words and the strength of his touch, she backed up a step, only to run into the solid body of Brandon behind her. She couldn't deny the hard press of his cock into the crack of her ass, nor the cream spilling from her pussy to coat her silky underwear.

"We both want you, Emma. Are you up for some hard lovin'?" Brandon asked, his hands running up and down her arms.

"W-what do you have in mind?"

Brandon swept her hair back from her neck and pressed a kiss to the soft spot just below her earlobe. "Ever had a man in your ass, honey?"

"N-no."

"Do you want to?"

"Oh God, yes." Heat swept over her cheeks at the admission of such a naughty thing. Anal sex? Good girls didn't give in to such torrid fantasies, did they? "I mean, I've thought about it and I...I'm curious."

"How about after we're done here tonight, you come back to the hotel with us? Nothin' has to happen you don't want, but between me and Beau, we can make your every fantasy a reality."

She sucked in a ragged breath and slowly blew it out in a small attempt to calm her racing heart. Could she really let both Brandon and Beau make love to her? *Make love, hell! It would be down and dirty sex and nothing more.* It would be a dream come true to have Brandon Tucker in her bed—and now that she knew there were two of them, the whole dream might be double the fun.

"What's it gonna be, darlin'?" Beau asked, standing in front of her and running his thumb over her bottom lip.

"Can I think about it?"

"Sure," Brandon replied, and Beau nodded. "We still have some work to do around here to get set up for tomorrow. Plus, I hear there's gonna be dancin' and drinkin' in a while."

"Yeah, there is. It's kind of a small party before the town gets flooded with tourists for the rodeo and all hell breaks loose tomorrow. I need to ask a question though." She licked her lips and took a deep breath. "Have you two done this before? Shared a girl I mean."

"A time or two," Beau answered. "You okay with that?"

"Does it matter? I mean, what you've done in the past, or what you'll do after you leave Red Rock doesn't matter a hill of beans to me. This is only for the here and now. No long term. No promises."

The looks passing between the twins gave her pause. Understanding and acceptance reflected in their eyes, but another, deeper emotion flickered for a moment and then disappeared. They wanted a quick down and dirty affair before they moved onto the next town. Didn't they?

She stepped from between them and headed for the tent. Thoughts danced in her mind and her body tingled with the promise in their words, but could she really have sex with both men?

* * * *

As the two of them watched her walk away, Beau couldn't believe how things were transpiring. The plan was to spend more time with Emma before they left, but he really hadn't been sure if she'd go for it. Yeah, the attraction and fire burned between the three of them. He felt it and he knew Brandon did too. If someone had told him he and Brandon would have a chance at one dark-haired, blue-eyed beauty last night, he'd have told them they'd lost their mind. The way she'd cussed at them and thrown them out of her house, he'd figured they'd blown their chance at anything with her without a whole lot of groveling.

"You think she'll go for it?" he asked Brandon.

"By the way she responded to being sandwiched between us, I'd say yeah. The whole thought of it intrigues her."

"Thinking about it has me hard enough to pound nails with my dick."

"Yeah. You and be both, brother," Brandon replied, pressing his hand down on his dick to try to relieve some of the pressure. "I want inside her ass so bad, I could come in my jeans right now."

"I bet her pussy tastes sweet. I want to eat her until she comes all over my face."

"We keep talkin' like this, Beau, and we'll both be headed for the bathroom to jack off."

"I know."

Brandon looked at his face and asked, "What the hell happened to your nose, anyhow?"

"Our little spitfire head-butted me," he replied, gingerly fingering the bridge of his nose.

"No shit!"

"Yeah. I followed her out here and grabbed her around the waist. I guess she didn't realize it was me, so she smashed her head into my nose. Damn near broke it."

"You're a walkin' wreck there, brother dear. You think you'll be up to makin' our little lady scream?" Brandon asked, slapping him on the back as they headed for the tent.

"Give me two minutes between those thighs, and she'll be more than screamin'."

"Yeah, yeah. I'll believe it when I see it."

"Is that a challenge, Brandon? See who can make her scream first or loudest?"

"Oh, I'm up for it. What'cha bettin'?"

"If I get her to come first with my name on her lips, you owe me one whole day alone with her."

Brandon rubbed his chin and grinned. "And if I make her come first screamin' *Brandon*, then I get one whole day alone with her."

They shook hands and Beau smiled. "You're on brother."

"But we can't tell Emma we're bettin' like this. She'll be pissed."

"Yeah. It'll be our secret."

When they reached the flap in the tent and walked inside, Beau's gaze automatically sought out the woman who had them both on edge. Emma stood at the back of the tent behind the beer taps, talking with Becky. As if she could feel his gaze, she turned to face them and smiled so sweetly, he wanted to grab her right then and run back to the hotel room. He needed to think of something else besides how hot she looked, how soft her hair had been when he'd held onto it while he kissed her, how luscious her lips tasted, and how nice her breast would feel in his palm. Going caveman on her wouldn't be the best move on his part, but damn! If she didn't quit looking at him like she wanted to eat him alive, he wouldn't be able to control himself much longer.

Think of somethin' man—anything besides her right now. Yeah, ridin' herd, stayin' on a bull for the full eight seconds, stackin' hay at our parents' place. Oh hell, this isn't workin' at all!

Several guys walked in with band equipment to set up for their show in about an hour, so he figured he'd help them. Maybe he'd stay so busy, he'd forget about Emma—for oh, about thirty seconds.

The sound of her laughter brought his attention back to her—not like it had strayed much anyway. Whether she laughed, moaned, sighed, or growled, he wanted to hear each sound as he made love to her.

Made love? Seriously? I'm gettin' in way over my head here. Hell, I've only know her two days. I need to

*think of this like it will actually be. Fuckin'. Having sex.
Doin' the horizontal mambo. Boinkin' her. Drilling her
ass. Eatin' her out and findin' out exactly how sweet her
cunt is. Okay. Yeah. Better.* He glanced at her and
caught her gaze on him—her eyes blazing blue, her
nipples hard points against her tank top, and a little
press of her thighs together telling him she was turned
on too. *Oh shit! I'm so screwed.*

* * * *

People flooded into the fairgrounds by the
truckload. Cars, pickups, four-wheelers, and every other
type of transportation one could think of found a spot to
park. The annual Founder's Day rodeo was winding up
for an all-out party. Tonight would be the opening
dance, the beer fest where the locals could come and
have some fun before the craziness started in the
morning.

"Wow. What a crowd already," Becky said,
manning the beer tap on the right side of the makeshift
bar.

"Yeah. I hope the tips are good tonight. I could use
the cash," Emma responded from the other end.

"Oh, please, Emma—you always rake it in every
time you play barmaid."

Her tip jar already showed signs of needing to be
emptied, and they'd only been serving for thirty
minutes. It helped that she wore a breast-hugging top
cut high to show off her belly button ring, jeans molded
to her hips, and a necklace dangling just above her
cleavage. Of course, she loved the looks she got from
Brandon and Beau the moment she stepped back inside
the tent after she'd changed her clothes. Both men

focused entirely on her, much to the chagrin of several other women in the room, and now they continued to sit off to her left at a table by themselves.

In a lull between customers, Becky came over to her side and nodded in the direction of her two men.

"So what's up with you and those two? Are you gonna move to the next step?"

"And what's the next step, Bec?" she asked sarcastically, letting Becky think what she would.

"Sex, of course." Becky's eyes widened and a small, dreamy smile curved her lips. "The thought of being sandwiched between those two hard bodies would make any red-blooded woman horny, and I've seen you shifting your stance over here." Becky laughed, and Emma blushed.

"Well, they did proposition me," she replied, absently wiping down the wooden plank serving as a bar.

Becky's eyebrows almost met her hair when she said, "Really? Wow! What'd you say?"

"Nothing yet. I told them I needed to think about it." She shrugged and glanced their way again, only to find both sets of brown eyes glued to her.

"What the hell is there to think about? I'd take either one, much less both."

"Oh please." Emma put both hands on her hips and snorted. "You're too hot for Seth to even think about being with another guy."

"I think about it, Emma. I think about it a lot, since Seth isn't an option for me."

She shook her head and sighed. "Substituting another man for the one you really want isn't right either."

"Hey! Can I get a beer?"

Both of them turned to face an obnoxious shout of a man at Becky's end of the bar. "Keep your boxers on, Mac. I'll be there in a second," Becky replied.

"Well hurry your sweet ass up. I need me another beer."

"You've probably already had too many, so just chill out a minute. Otherwise I won't serve you."

"The hell you won't, girl. Do I need to beat your ass for you? Maybe you like it a little rough. I bet I can oblige."

Fury and indignation rushed through Emma. Smartass, drunk men pissed her off. "You'd better shut your trap or I'll—"

"You'll what, Emma?" he asked, infuriating her further.

"Enough, Mac," Seth said, stopping next to the tap. "You're done for the night, buddy. No more for you."

"Fuck you, Seth Reardon. My buddies and I keep you in business. Now I want another beer, and I want little miss hoity-toity over there to serve it to me between her breasts. I've got a hankerin' to lick those pretty little tips with the end of my tongue."

The next thing Emma realized, Beau and Brandon stood on either side of the intoxicated man, and the place went silent when Seth pulled back his fist and knocked MacKenzie to the ground.

"If you ever fuckin' talk about my woman like that again, Mac, you won't be walkin' for several weeks, 'cause I'll break your legs for you. And don't bother to come back into my bar. From now on, you can drink somewhere else." Seth motioned for Beau and Brandon to escort MacKenzie from the tent amongst the round of applause from the rest of the people in the place.

"Did you hear that?" Emma whispered in Becky's ear. "He called you his woman."

Tears welled in her friend's gaze, and before Emma couldn't say anything more, Becky turned and fled the tent.

Seth watched from several feet away until Emma went over to him and said, "If you want her, you need to go after her. Enough of this crap. Tell her how you feel, Seth, otherwise you might as well give up right now."

After a moment he nodded and followed Becky outside.

"Damn stubborn men," Emma grumbled, taking her place at the tap again and started serving customers.

The line grew to unbelievable lengths until she noticed the women shifting to the other end of the bar. She glanced to her right and about dropped the cup in her hand when she saw Brandon serving beer after beer. He looked her way, winked and smiled.

"Hey folks! I've got an idea," Beau shouted from the raised stage at the other end of the bar. "How about a friendly competition between Emma and Brandon?"

The roar of approval made her ears ring, but she wasn't sure she wanted anything to do with a competition Beau might come up with. It appeared she didn't have a choice when his voice rose above the crowd.

"On one end of the bar we have local beauty Emma Weston. Dark haired, big blue eyes and cleavage deep enough to make any man's mouth water. On the other end we have Brandon Tucker, country crooner, handsome devil in disguise—so be careful ladies—an all-around ladies' man. We're gonna put up tip jars for both on the table there, and for the next hour while the band plays, all tips will go to Charlene Campbell's folks for her hospital bills. The two contestants can do whatever it takes to make the tips. Kiss, touch… What do you say?"

Is he serious? All eyes focused on her and Brandon.

A wickedly sexy grin lifted the corners of Brandon's mouth, and he took the several steps between them to close the gap. One arm slipped around her waist, and he pulled her toward him. "What do you say, honey? You game?"

"Uh, sure. I guess. It's to help out Charlene, so I'll do whatever."

Fire danced in the brown depths of his eyes, and she had a bad feeling about how this would play out. Somehow, she got the idea that whether she won or lost, Brandon Tucker was about to turn her world upside down.

"How about we make our own little side bet?"

Shivers rolled down her spine, and she took a deep breath to calm her racing heart. "What do you have in mind?" she whispered in a choked voice.

"Let's see," he murmured. "If I win, Beau and I get your company exclusively whenever we want it, to do with as we please—including you naked and at our mercy—for the rest of the time we're in town."

She swallowed hard. "And what if I win?"

"Name your poison, honey."

Did she dare ask for what she wanted? If she lost, she'd still get this gnawing ache inside her filled by two heavenly looking guys, one of whom she'd lusted after for way too long and the other, his identical twin.

The need to see if the real Brandon Tucker could drop the megastar attitude and be the man any girl would love to fall for spurred her on. Beau would do what she asked without a second thought—with his caring personality, he could do no less—but Brandon?

Leaning toward him so only he could hear her words, she whispered, "You'll give half of everything you make over the next year to charity."

Chapter Five

"You drive a hard bargain, baby, but you're on," Brandon replied and then kissed her hard on the mouth.

Her whole body tingled under the pressure of his kiss. She arched into his embrace and wrapped her arms around his neck, giving in to the heat of his mouth and the longing inside her. Slowly the wolf whistles and catcalls penetrated her foggy brain enough for her to push against his chest.

"Let the games begin," she whispered and then stepped back to take her place at the tap. "You do know how to handle that thing, right, big man?"

"A beer tap? I'm a cowboy, honey. I've been handlin' beer since before you were born."

"I doubt it." She let her gaze run from the top of his Stetson to the toes of his boots. "Besides, I got somethin' you ain't got, hot man."

"Oh?" he asked, splaying his fingers and cracking his knuckles as he prepared to start pouring.

"Yeah. These," she said, wiggling her breasts and tugging her top down far enough only the nipples and the bottom of her breasts were covered. Then she tucked the hem of her shirt into the elastic bottom of the built in bra. "Bring it on boys!"

The band tuned up and let rip a saucy beer drinking song, and the race was on. Men drooled on her, kissed her, and she even let a few feel a little, but the tip jar on Brandon's side stayed pretty much neck and neck with hers. She watched as he passed out tongue-melting kisses in exchange for lots and lots of cash in his tip jar. The burning ache in her chest from watching him fondle practically every woman in the place never went away. Beau soothed her a little with kisses and touches of his own, but she felt like a third of her was missing.

At the end of the hour, Beau pulled both tip jars and took them up on the stage to be counted.

"Any last bits of change or bills anyone wants to add to either jar? They look pretty close, and I know every little bit will go to help Charlene get better."

The crowd groaned, and one guy yelled, "Hell, I'm already flat damn broke, but all the touches and kisses I got from Emma was worth every dime."

"Chill out, John," she shouted from her spot at the taps. She nervously watched while Beau and Becky counted the money, not sure if she wanted to win or lose.

"This unbelievable, folks. I think someone was keeping count while the whole thing went on. The totals are so close, it's amazing. The grand total of both jars together comes out to four hundred twenty-three dollars and fourteen cents."

The crowd erupted in shouts, high-fives, and wild hugs.

"Now for the winner. Brandon and Emma, you two need to come up here for this."

"Come on, honey. Take your punishment like a lady," Brandon said with a wicked grin.

Emma let Brandon take her hand as they made their way to the stage. When they stood side-by-side in front of the crowd, butterflies erupted in her stomach, and she silently prayed she'd lose. The thought of being at their mercy for the entire time they were in town tied her insides into knots.

Beau stood between her and Brandon and worked the crowd into a frenzy before he calmed them with a raised hand. "All right, all right. We have a winner. Drum roll, please." After several moments and complete silence from the crowd, he said, "The winner is..." He shifted his glance from her to Brandon and back. "Brandon! By thirty-five cents."

"It was my thirty-five cents!" a blonde in the front shouted. "I should get an extra kiss."

"Come on up here, sweet thing," Brandon said, and the blonde jumped up on stage. It took him all of two seconds to plant a wet kiss on her painted lips and her to stick her tongue down his throat, much to the delight of the crowd around them.

Emma couldn't stand to watch it.

As she jumped down from the stage and headed back to the beer taps, she could feel the tears behind her eyes. *I will not cry. I will not cry. What do I care if he kisses someone else?*

"Whoa, honey. Where are you runnin' off to?" Brandon asked, grabbing her hand before she reached the back of the tent.

"I need some air," she whispered, pulling her hand out of his grasp and dashing outside.

"Emma!"

She rounded the back of the stock barn and slipped into the shadows, hoping he wouldn't find her until she'd had a chance to come to terms with the green-eyed monster rearing its ugly head. Neither Brandon nor Beau belonged to her, so why these crazy thoughts and feelings bombarded her heart, she didn't know.

"Come on, baby. I know you're back here."

Refusing to let him comfort her, she stayed silent, hoping he would give up and go back to the tent. The thought of giving herself to the two of them made her pussy ache and throb with need so strong, it almost brought her to her knees, but she had to keep her heart out of the fray, otherwise she'd never survive.

"I'll leave you alone for a bit, Emma, but don't stay out here long. If you aren't back inside the tent in ten minutes, I'm coming out here looking for you."

His silhouette disappeared back around the front of the barn, and she sighed in relief. She couldn't get involved with these two past the few days they'd be in Red Rock. If she did, she'd be left brokenhearted and alone.

Shoring up her pride and building the wall back up around her heart, she headed for the tent, knowing if she didn't make an appearance shortly, he would come after her. She reached it only to find him and Beau both standing just inside the flap.

"You okay, darlin'?" Beau asked, wiping a lingering tear from her cheek.

"I'm fine. I needed a minute. That's all." She glanced at Brandon and then back to Beau. "Did he tell you the contents of our side bet?"

"Yeah, but don't worry, Emma. You don't have to do anythin' you don't want to."

"I made the bet. I'll live up to it," she answered, pulling back her shoulders. "But we still have a few hours left here. Everyone will wander home about midnight."

"Will you dance with me?" Brandon asked, taking her hand and bringing it to his lips. "I want to feel your body pressed to mine."

She took a deep breath and nodded. Moments later, she found herself held tightly to his broad chest, his palm at the small of her back scorching the bare skin above her waistband and his hot breath on her ear.

"Why did you run off?"

"I told you. I needed some air."

"You know the girl meant nothin'. It was just a kiss."

"With her tongue down your throat."

"Ah. I see."

"You see what, Brandon?" she asked, moving back far enough she could look into his eyes. "You don't belong to me, so I can't tell you what to do with other women. You can kiss or fondle whoever you want."

"But Beau and I belong to you like you belong to us…for now."

"For now is all I want. I don't need any kind of relationship. I've got school, my horse, and my family. Men come and go."

"You sound pretty hard-hearted, honey."

"I've seen my share of heartbreak, Brandon, and I refuse to let anyone get that close to me again. Short-term affairs, one-night stands, and no commitment is the way to go." Her heart cracked at the lie. She knew the life-style Brandon and Beau led, with the constant touring and driving from one side of the country to the other, left no time for any kind of real relationship.

"Do you want to tell me about it?"

"No."

"Maybe after some time you'll trust me enough to tell me," he whispered, his hot lips against the side of her neck.

"It's over and done with, and it doesn't matter anymore. I'm not goin' into this thing with you and

Beau with my heart on my sleeve. It's gonna be a few days of raunchy sex, good times, and hard lovin'. Nothing more. You're a fantasy come to life for me, times two, but that's it."

It sounded all good and strong, but her heart wasn't swayed, especially when Brandon slid his lips to the spot right below her ear and sucked on it. Her knees wobbled and blood rushed in her ears, but she convinced herself it was all a physical reaction to his nearness.

"Mind if I cut in?" Beau asked from behind her.

"Of course I mind," Brandon growled. "But since we're bound to share her, we might as well start now." He stepped back, brushed his lips over hers, and then headed for the bar.

"What's up, darlin'?"

"Nothin', why?"

"You seemed in an awful big hurry to get out of here a little bit ago."

"Not you too," she snapped, rolling her eyes. "It's nothin'. I told Brandon the same thing. It's nothin'."

"Then why the tears when you came back in?"

"All right. You want the truth? I'll give it to you. It bothered me when he kissed that girl, and it shouldn't have. Neither of you mean anythin' to me except some fun sex for the next several days, so it shouldn't bug me."

Beau ran a finger down her cheek and across her bottom lip. "You don't sound so convinced, Emma."

"Well I am." She saw Becky, waved to her, and said, "Sorry. I have to go finish manning the beer taps until everyone goes home."

"Okay," he replied, letting her go.

She could feel both sets of brown eyes watching her every step as she made her way back to the bar, never letting up until things wound down and everyone started going home. Beau and Brandon helped Seth, Becky, and her clean up the area and put everything away while the band cleared out.

Seth got up on the stage and whistled to get everyone's attention. "Let's call it a night, folks. Beau. Brandon. Thank you both for all your help tonight and I'm sure the extra money we raised will be very much appreciated by Charlene's family. We'll get the word out about tomorrow's acoustic set, and hopefully we can rake is a lot more."

"Let's hope so," Brandon replied, tucking both hands into the front pockets of his jeans. "I can only imagine what Charlene and her family are going through."

"How long are you guys going to be in town?" Seth asked, stepping off the stage.

"We aren't sure. The mechanic couldn't tell us how long it would be before the parts got here. Could be a few days or a couple of weeks."

"Weeks?" Emma squeaked and then cleared her throat. *Weeks? This isn't good. How in the hell am I going to be at their beck and call for weeks and still keep my heart intact?*

Beau's sexy smile had her squeezing her thighs together to ease the ache in her pussy. Soon. She just had to get away from Becky and Seth.

"Can you give me a ride home, Emma?" Becky asked.

"Um, no. I have an errand to run. Seth can run you home, can't he?"

"Sure. No problem," Seth replied and Becky gave her a nasty look.

She'd been so wrapped up in everything going on between her, Brandon, and Beau, she hadn't gotten a chance to talk to Becky about what had happened earlier when Seth followed her outside. Unfortunately, when the two of them had returned, nothing appeared to have changed. They still managed to avoid being close together, but Emma thought there might be subtle changes no one else noticed. She knew her friends, and it seemed Becky spent a little more time close to Seth, touching his sleeve when they talked and smiling a little more. She really hoped the two of them could work things out.

After Seth and Becky drove off, Emma stood next to her mother's old car. With her truck in the shop, she had to have something to drive, and her dad had insisted she use the old car since it just sat at the house, unused. It felt kind of weird driving it, though, since her mother's death two years earlier.

Silence enveloped the three of them as they stood there looking at each other, each waiting for someone else to make the first move.

"So. What exactly is this bet going to entail?" she asked, her stomach knotting up nervously like a wad of tissue.

"You'll see. Do you want to follow us back to the hotel so you have your car there?" Brandon asked, wrapping a lock of her hair around his finger.

"I guess," she replied, pulling her hair out of his grasp and opening the door to the car. "Lead the way, gentlemen."

Beau flashed her a wicked grin and opened the rental car. "Let's go, Brandon. I got me a hard-on screaming for a sweet pussy."

Emma shook her head, wondering if she was losing her mind, letting these two anywhere near her. How she would be able to come out of this without losing her heart, she didn't know.

Fifteen minutes later, she pulled into the nicest hotel in Red Rock—which really wasn't saying much, but Cade had money invested in it, so she knew the inside could rival some of the nicest hotels in the big cities like Los Angeles and New York. Cade and his big money investors had converted a large old stone building in town and renovated it to the hilt. They could charge an arm and a leg for rooms, since Red Rock wasn't far from the interstate and the huge recreation lake sat mere feet from the back of the building. She figured Brandon could afford one of the suites if he wanted to. It would be interesting to see what room they'd chosen.

Gilded mirrors lined the lobby. Soft deep red brocade covered all the chairs, and marble slabs made up the floor. Crystal chandeliers hung every so many feet along the ceiling, bouncing multi-colored shards of light around the room. Large ferns graced the corners, and a huge black marble counter separated the check-in people from the guests.

Hopefully she wouldn't run into anyone she knew going through the lobby. If word got back to her dad, he'd kill her. It didn't matter that she had passed the age of consent at least six years ago. At the age of twenty-four, she knew what she wanted, and right now it came in the very enticing package of Beau and Brandon Tucker.

"Miss Emma, to what do we owe this surprise visit?"

Emma froze at the voice and slowly turned to face Aiden, the night manager of the hotel and a long-time friend of Cade's, walking toward where she stood in the middle of the lobby. Lucky for her, Beau and Brandon hadn't made an appearance behind her—yet.

"Hey Aiden. How's business?"

"Not bad. I'm sure the rodeo will be bringing in a ton of people starting tomorrow. We're already almost full. Are you meeting someone here?"

"Um…yeah. A friend."

"Ah," he replied, nodding. "Are they coming in for the rodeo?"

"No. Not necessarily." She pulled her bottom lip between her teeth and tried to think of the easiest explanation for her appearance at the hotel without giving away her plans for a threesome rendezvous.

"There are you, darlin'," Beau said, coming up behind her and putting his arm around her waist. "We thought we'd lost you."

"I'm right here," she replied, her overly bright tone grating on her nerves. *Damn it! Do I have to sound so high-schoolish?*

"Evening, sir." Aiden stuck out his hand for Beau to shake. "I'm Aiden Moss. Night manager."

"Nice to meet you Mr. Moss."

"Um, we should go, Beau."

"We need to wait for Brandon. He's parkin' the rental car."

Aiden's eyebrow shot up as he glanced at her and then back to Beau. "Brandon Tucker? I saw his name on the guest roster. It's nice to have you and your brother with us, Mr. Tucker."

"You know, there is one thing you can do for me." Beau tapped his finger to his lip and narrowed his eyes.

"Just name it, sir."

"Send up a bottle of champagne, some strawberries, and whipped cream from the kitchen."

Emma's whole body hummed when she heard Beau's request. Did they plan to eat off her? Or eat her, period? *God, I hope so.*

"Certainly, sir. I'll take care of it right now. Any particular brand of champagne?"

"No. Just somethin' nice and smooth. Brandon and I don't want our lady friend here to think we're some backwoods country boys."

"Of course not," Aiden replied. "Nice to see you again, Emma. I'll mention it to Cade when I see him."

"No!" Emma yelled as Aiden turned to head toward the desk.

He spun back to face her with a quizzical look.

"I mean, I'll tell him I saw you, Aiden. I'm sure he'll be pleased at how well you're running your shift here at the hotel, but don't bother calling him. I'm sure I'll see him tomorrow."

"All right. Enjoy your evening."

As she watched Aiden disappear toward the kitchen, Brandon came through the doors and joined them.

"I figured you two would have already gone upstairs and gotten started strippin'," Brandon said, taking her hand and kissing the palm. "Not changin' your mind, are you, Emma?"

"Uh, no."

"We ran into someone who knows Cade and Emma. The night manager here. I have him sending up some fun items to try."

"Wonderful. Shall we?" Brandon asked, pulling her along toward the elevators. "I can't wait to get you alone." He glanced at his brother and grinned. "Or should I say I can't wait to get you between us?"

Shivers raced down her spine, and goose bumps pimpled her skin as a picture of her sandwiched between Beau and Brandon raced across her mind. Heat spread through her body, centered low in her belly, and her pussy throbbed with need.

Within moments, they stood outside of a suite on the upper floor of the hotel. Even though Cade was a partner in the hotel, she'd never seen the inside of one of these rooms. They were expensive and luxurious. After Brandon opened the door, she caught her breath in a gasp. The room screamed money. Gold and crystal chandeliers hung from the ceiling and smaller versions hung as sconces on the walls. A kitchen big enough to put her mom's to shame sat to her left, and a doorway to the right revealed two of the biggest beds she'd ever seen.

"Wow," she whispered.

"You've never been up here?" Beau asked, wrapping his arms around her from behind.

"No. Cade invests in this place, but I've never seen the suites. This is amazing. I wonder what the bathroom looks like."

"Come on. I'll show you," Brandon said, taking her hands and pulling her out of Beau's embrace.

The bathroom took her breath away. A huge shower took up one whole wall, with adjustable heads to make water spray in several directions at once. The tile squares were black with gold swirled through each one. The vanity had two sinks and ran almost the entire length of the opposite wall, and she couldn't stop staring at the bathtub.

"Oh my God! Look at the size of the tub!"

"I know. Cool, huh," Brandon replied, slipping in behind her. "I would love to put tons of bubbles in there and slide under the water with you, caressing every inch of your skin with my hands and sliding my palms over your breasts until your nipples turn to diamond-hard points just begging for my mouth."

She leaned back against his chest and let his words float to her ears as her eyes closed.

"I'd lift you up on the side of the tub there and bury my face in your pussy. I can't wait to see how you taste, Emma. Salty goodness or sweet like candy? I bet you're so sweet, I'll be hard pressed not to gorge myself on you."

The moment his palm touched bare skin, her pussy flooded with need so strong, blood seemed to hum through her veins. Within seconds, he had her bare breast in his hand, caressing the flesh, but avoiding her aching nipple.

"That's it, baby, relax."

The hand not already occupied flicked open the button on her jeans, and she heard the low rasp of the zipper as he pulled it down.

"God, you're so hot, Emma," he whispered as his free hand slipped down under the elastic of her thong to dive between her thighs. "You're wet for me—for us. So slick and blistering hot. Your pussy is on fire."

Her whole body trembled with each pass of his fingers.

"Hey bro, save some for me," Beau said from the doorway.

"Just gettin' her warmed up," Brandon replied, pulling his hands away and stepping back.

When she opened her eyes, the drop-dead gorgeous come-kiss-me smile on Brandon's lips reminded her of some of the pictures she'd seen of him on the web and in magazines. He'd always had a pretty blonde on his arm, and suddenly she felt a bit self-conscious. Although she considered herself fairly pretty, she knew she couldn't hold a candle to some of the model-thin and big-boobed women she'd seen him with. "Um. I'll be right out, guys. I need to use the facilities."

"Sure, darlin'," Beau said, leaving her alone.

"Don't take too long, baby. My cock is so hard right now, I'll be hard pressed to keep from coming before I'm even inside your hot pussy," Brandon added and then stepped out.

The moment the door closed behind them, Emma took a deep breath and closed her eyes.

I'm crazy. How can I possibly satisfy two men? Hell, I don't even know if I'll be able to satisfy one of them. When she opened her eyes again, the woman in the mirror stared back with a look of terror in her eyes. She'd never thought of herself as gorgeous or anything. Pretty, yeah, but plain. How could she possibly think to hold not one, but two gorgeous men's attention? *Brandon is so hot, he has a different woman every night, I imagine. And Beau? He's sweet, funny, and ohmigod sizzling.*

"Well, the only way I'll find out is to jump in with both feet." After she used the toilet, she quickly rinsed her mouth, checked her teeth for anything funky stuck between them, fluffed her hair a little, and smoothed down her shirt. *Silly. Your clothes will be off two seconds after you walk back into that room.*

After a fortifying breath, she opened the door, only to be met by bookend men with their arms crossed over their chests and wicked gleams in their eyes.

Beau frowned and stepped next to her. "You okay, darlin'? You looked scared to death."

"I'm fine, Beau. Just nervous, I guess. I've never done anythin' like this before."

"Had sex?"

She playfully punched him in the ribs. "No, silly. Been with two guys at once. I'm not sure what to do."

"We'll take care of everythin', honey," Brandon said, sliding in on her other side and wrapping his arm around her waist.

The two of them led her to the side of the bed, sandwiching her between them with Beau in front and Brandon warming her from the back. A nervous flutter started in her stomach when Brandon inched her tank top up from inside the waistband of her jeans. The warmth of his fingers on the bare flesh of her waist sent the butterflies she harbored in her belly up to take flight. His lips caressed her shoulder, inching their way in a slow, delicious slide from the curve of shoulder to a spot on her neck she didn't realize had such luscious consequences.

"She likes that, Brandon," Beau said, sliding the straps down with his thumbs. "No bra, huh?"

"Built into my top," she murmured, wanting him to hurry so she could feel his mouth on her breast.

"Convenient. Do you want my mouth, Emma, darlin'? Your nipples are poking out, begging for me to lick on them."

A soft moan escaped her lips as she tipped her head to the side and back onto Brandon's shoulder, giving him better access to her neck. The moment the top eased off her breasts and exposed her taut nipples to the cool air, they bunched tight. Beau licked the tip of the right one, making her whole body tremble.

"Nice," Beau whispered, before sucking the tip into his mouth.

Her knees wobbled, and one of the twins' arms went around her waist to steady her, although she couldn't have said whose if her life depended on it. Blood rushed in her ears, and she could have sworn that at the very moment Beau sucked on her nipple, the tip of her breast and her clit were somehow connected. The tingling and throbbing she felt exploded into heart-thumping, pulsating need as cream spilled out of her pussy, wetting the silky thong between her thighs. "Please."

"Tell us what you want, honey," Brandon murmured against her neck.

"Suck harder, Beau."

"My pleasure, darlin'."

The pull of his mouth on her nipple and the nip of Brandon's teeth on her earlobe had her body screaming to move, but she couldn't decide which direction to go to get more stimulation.

"Please. I need..." Beau's mouth left her breast, and she groaned in frustration. "No, don't stop."

His lips nibbled at the corners of her mouth right before his tongue slid inside to tangle with hers. Brandon did his own exploration of her spine, shoulders, arms and waist as he reached around, unsnapped her jeans, and lowered the zipper. Cool air hit her skin as the pants and panties pooled at her ankles, and Brandon nudged her to step out by lifting her foot and removing one boot at a time. The moment she stood completely bare from the waist down,

Brandon's hands crawled up the insides of her calves as his lips danced over the flesh of her butt, nipping softly at each cheek.

Beau lifted his head and growled, "Damn, woman. You burn me up with those lips, but we need to get the rest of this off." He lifted the tank top over her head and tossed it aside. "Now where were we?"

"On the bed, honey," Brandon instructed, walking her backward until her knees hit the mattress.

Her breath caught in her throat as she watched both Beau and Brandon do a little striptease for her. Each had a smattering of hair trailing from one nipple to the other across a broad chest and then in a sexy path down until it disappeared into the waistband of his jeans. The bulge each sported threatened to rip the seams apart. Hot damn!

"You like what you see, darlin'?"

"Oh, hell yeah," she whispered, capturing her bottom lip between her teeth. "More, please."

Beau unbuttoned his jeans and slowly drew the zipper down as her heart rate seemed to triple with each inch of his cock revealed. Long and thick, with deep veins running from base to head, the sight of it made her mouth water to taste the pearly essence of his desire clinging to the top. When the denim fell to the floor, she took a ragged breath, glancing at Brandon to see how far he'd undressed before looking back at Beau.

"You keep lookin' at me like that, and I won't be able to wait," Beau said, his eyes blazing with passion and need.

She licked her suddenly dry lips. "Like what?"

"With those big blue eyes and come-kiss-me lips. I want to lick you all over."

"Then do it cowboy," she murmured, holding out her hand and waiting for him to take it before drawing him down on top of her.

Moments later, Brandon crawled onto the bed beside them. The warmth of his skin heated every spot it touched. With his left leg tossed over hers, he effectively spread her thighs open for whatever came next, and what came next was Beau's feathery touch on the insides of her legs. Goosebumps followed the light skimming of his fingers from ankle to thigh, but he avoided the places she needed him most. Her thighs quivered and her pussy throbbed, waiting for him to touch it. She almost screamed when he avoided her pussy in favor of running his fingers over her stomach.

"You have magnificent tits, honey. Nice rosy nipples just begging for attention," Brandon whispered, running his lips over her shoulder.

She cupped both breasts and lifted them in invitation—to which man, she didn't care. "I want your tongue, both of you." A purr escaped her lips when first Brandon and then Beau each took a nipple into his mouth and sucked. "Yes." Beau flicked her right nipple with the tip of his tongue, bringing a tortured moan to her lips as Brandon encircled the left. "So good."

Beau released her breast and blew a cool stream of air over the nipple, humming his appreciation when the peak stiffened and beaded into a hard point.

Unable to stop the emotions and desires flooding her body, she begged for more with soft whimpers and tortured groans until she felt one of the twins nudge her thighs apart.

"Ah, God!" she screamed as the first lick touched her pussy. Her back arched when a wet mouth closed over a nipple and pulled it deep into the warm cavern.

The wicked tongue between her pussy lips flicked, swirled, and speared, changing the pace so she couldn't zero in on any one thing to drive her over the edge of climax. Sensations swamped her, bombarding her from every direction. Soft nips of teeth on one nipple, the pinch of fingers on the opposite one, and the warm flick of the torturous tongue built the desire inside her to a fever pitch. Her body wasn't her own. They controlled the craving, spiraling want until she quivered uncontrollably. The tingling started in her toes, rushing up her legs to center low in her belly.

"Please," she begged. "I need—"

"We know what you need, honey," Brandon whispered against her lips, leaving the cooling wet spot on her nipple open to the sensations of his chest hair sliding across the tip.

"She's so sweet, Brandon. Wait until you taste this," Beau said from between her thighs. "I could eat her all day."

"Stop talking, Beau, and do it. Make me come. God, I can't stand this. Please."

"Demanding little thing, aren't you?" Brandon pinched her nipple between his thumb and first finger.

The sharpness of the tug sent heat spiraling through her system and straight to her clit.

"Yes, yes, yes," she panted, tossing her head from side to side.

He slid his tongue over the peak and then bit it at the same time Beau flicked her clit in a quick figure eight, sending her climax washing over her in a huge wave of sensation. Tingles raced up her legs. A sharp burst of heat slammed through her belly, and she screamed as her body convulsed in a mind-numbing climax.

"Oh God! Beau!"

When the whooshing sound cleared her ears, she heard a chuckle from between her legs. Beau continued to slowly lick her clit, holding her desire at a steady pull until she came completely down from her first climax. She slowly opened her eyes to see Brandon staring down at her with a frown.

"What? Did I do somethin' wrong?" she asked, afraid she'd caused a major issue for some reason.

"Nothin'," he snapped, rolling away from her.

"It's not nothin', Brandon." She grabbed his bicep to stop him from moving further away as Beau sat up and crossed his arms over his chest. "Talk to me. You can't frown at me like that—like I screwed up bad—and then hold it in."

"He hates losing," Beau replied with a smirk on his sexy lips.

"Losing at what? I didn't think we had a contest going on here."

"Promise you won't get mad?" Beau asked.

Fear made her stomach clench. What weren't they telling her? "I don't like when sentences start that way, but fine, I promise not to get mad."

"We made a little side bet between the two of us after you almost broke my nose outside the beer tent."

"And?"

"Whoever's name you screamed when you came would get one whole day alone with you," Brandon explained.

"And I won," Beau said.

Irritation cleared the remaining desire from her body for the moment. The way these two made everything a game between them was really beginning to piss her off. "Is this always a game between you two? Because you know, I'm not really into this competition shit. I'm here with both of you. I want to be with both of you, not just you, Beau, and not just you, Brandon." She stretched out on the bed and spread her thighs. "Your turn to make me scream your name, Brandon."

The wicked gleam in his eyes and the sexy smile on his lips told her she had handled the situation correctly, but what would happen later on, when they got around to the fucking part? Which one would actually penetrate her body with his impressive cock? Or would she take both?

Chapter Six

It was like Brandon couldn't move fast enough to get between her thighs. She smothered a giggle with her hand when he dove over her leg to wiggle into position, but with the first thrust of his tongue into her vagina, she closed her eyes and moaned. Having two men focused on her needs drove her to the brink of a mind-blowing orgasm the minute Brandon touched her with his tongue.

"Open your eyes, darlin'," Beau coaxed, sliding onto the bed near her head. "I wanna see those baby blues when he makes you come."

The wide head of his cock bobbed against his stomach, looking hard enough to be uncomfortable. She reached out and encircled the engorged rod with her hand, stroking up and down a few times.

"Don't stop, darlin'. It feels awesome."

A low growl brought her glance to his face. Strains of concentration crinkled his eyebrows, and he licked his lips several times, as if fighting to hold himself together.

With a small tug on his cock, she managed to convey what she wanted, encouraging him to scoot close enough to line up his rigid shaft with her mouth. She slowly licked up the length and smiled when goose bumps sprung up on his thighs. After several swirls around the purple head, she swiped at the pre-cum with her tongue, tasting the salty, musky essence of Beau.

"Oh yeah. That's it. Suck me," he groaned, shifting his hips closer.

The length of flesh disappeared between her lips, and she felt the vibration of his moan when she whirled her tongue around him. Concentration grew difficult with Brandon between her thighs, licking and sucking her clit between his lips and spearing her vagina with his tongue.

Suck swallow. Suck swallow. *Make it good for Beau.* Each pass of his cock between her lips and into her mouth met with her hand coming up from the bottom to give him the most pleasure she could. She palmed his balls, rolling them between her fingers.

Releasing Beau's cock from her mouth, she moaned, "God, Brandon. Make me come. I need to come so bad."

"In a bit, honey. I'm enjoying this," Brandon replied, slipping two fingers inside her pussy while another finger played with her back hole, not quite penetrating the virgin space. Round and round he went, teasing the puckered ring until she relaxed and pushed her butt back against his finger, begging him to slip it inside.

"Do you want this?" he asked, spreading her juices from her pussy to her asshole. He pushed one digit slowly past the ring of muscle, and then two.

"*Yes.*"

The slow pump of his fingers burned at first, but within moments the pain turned to the most incredible pleasure she'd ever felt. Different sensations bombarded her from both holes. The tingling in her in ass spread to her pussy, igniting the fire quickly spreading through her body. More juice dripped from her vagina to coat his fingers, lubricating the slide.

"Mmm," she hummed, not letting Beau's cock leave her mouth now that she'd engulfed his rock-hard flesh again.

Beau's breathing sped up, matching her own as she fought her impending climax, not wanting the wicked sensations to stop yet. Hot spurts of cum coated her tongue and spilled down her throat with each thrust of Beau's hips and every groan he released. Brandon nipped at her clit, causing her own orgasm to scream through her body so unexpectedly, she barely had time to breathe and remember not to bite down on Beau before she released his softening cock and screamed Brandon's name.

"Beautiful, honey. Absolutely, beautiful," Brandon said, scooping up some of her cream and licking his fingers clean. He glanced up at Beau. "Grab me a condom, brother."

Beau grabbed a foil wrapped package from the nightstand and tossed it to Brandon. "Give me a second to catch my breath, honey, and we'll get this party started."

"I plan to start without you, Beau," Brandon said as he flipped her over on her stomach, brought her up on her knees, and slowly pushed his cock into her pussy. "Oh, hell yeah."

The glide of his cock felt like heaven and hell. She wanted everything—every inch deep inside.

Pushing her butt up and back, she heard him hiss, and she smiled. "Fuck me, Brandon. Give it to me. All of it."

With a hard snap of his hips, he drove the full length into her, hitting the special spot that made her purr like a kitten.

"Yes, yes! Right there."

"You have such a sweet, sweet pussy. You feel amazin', Emma. Tight, hot and wet."

"Brandon?"

"Yeah?"

"Shut up."

He chuckled and picked up the pace of his thrusts. "Better, honey?"

"Oh yeah. Fuck me hard."

She glanced to her side to see Beau stroking his returning erection with his palm and watching Brandon screw her brains out. Her whole body hummed with the knowledge both men wanted her like this, even if it turned into a short term thing. "Your turn next, Beau, so don't stroke it too hard."

"Not on your life, darlin'. I can't wait to get inside you."

"Squeeze those pussy muscles around me, baby. Yeah, just like that," Brandon said, shoving his cock in and out of her so hard, she had to spread her hands apart so she wouldn't scoot across the mattress.

Brandon slipped his hand around her stomach and rubbed her clit with his thumb, spiking her desire to boiling as he continued to pound into her until the orgasm rolled over her like a tidal wave. Two more body-slamming thrusts and Brandon climaxed with a tortured groan.

When Brandon withdrew from her pussy she collapsed onto her stomach and then rolled over onto her back. Her whole body hummed from the mind-numbing climaxes she'd had over the last hour, and they weren't through with her yet. Beau sported a hard-on worth drooling over, and she wanted all the yummy length deep inside her.

"You wouldn't believe how hot it is watching him fuck you, Emma. God, you're beautiful when you come," Beau whispered, brushing the sweaty hair from her face as her breathing slowed. "You ready for me, darlin'?"

She skimmed her fingers over his handsome face. "More than ready, Beau. I've wanted this from the moment you brushed your thumb over my lip at the accident. But can I ask somethin'?"

"Anythin'."

"I want you to make love to me. Slow and easy, face to face."

The smile spreading across his lips lit up the room. "My pleasure."

* * * *

Beau felt like a fist squeezed his heart. Make love to her? He would. Savor the time they had together? He would. Hold them close to his heart when they drove away? He would. Get over Emma Weston? Probably not in this lifetime.

The moment he slipped his cock into her welcoming warmth, he knew he'd found home. Tears glistened on her lashes, and one slipped from her eye into her hair.

"Am I hurtin' you, darlin'?"

"No," she whispered, taking a sharp breath. "It feels fantastic. Don't stop."

Her whole body shuddered when she clamped her pussy muscles around his throbbing cock. Holding still wasn't an option anymore when she lifted her hips and wrapped those magnificent legs around him. The slow glide of his cock in and out of her heat had him on the verge of climax within seconds, but he shoved it back down. He wasn't some randy teenager without any control.

The temptation of her lips drew him. He pressed his mouth against hers and ran his tongue over the surface of her lips, coaxing the response he wanted from her. Her sigh sent shivers down his spine. The brush of her tongue along his drew his balls up tight against his groin. If he didn't hurry her along, he'd blow long before she did—and that wasn't acceptable to him. With a swivel of his hips and a faster pace, she started to whimper into his mouth. He reached between them and raked his fingernail over her clit. Her pussy quivered as her climax built and he could feel every clasp of her pussy and every quiver of the walls of her vagina. When her orgasm hit, he careened over the edge right along with her.

Beau shuddered several times while their mutual climax cooled. Realization hit him square in the chest. He'd forgotten the condom. "Shit, Emma. God, I'm sorry. I've never ever lost control like that before," he said, dropping his forehead to her shoulder.

"What?" she asked, running her fingers through his hair and down his back.

"I forgot the condom." He rolled off of her and threw his arm across his eyes. "Damn it!"

"What's wrong, Beau?" Brandon asked from the bathroom doorway.

He'd completely forgotten his brother was even in the room while he made love to Emma, but now he felt like shit. How in the hell had he forgotten to put on the condom?

"Beau?"

"Yeah?" he replied, not meeting her gaze. Guilt and remorse clouded the excitement of making love to Emma.

"I'm clean, and I'm on the pill."

Leave it to her to make him feel better. He should be the one comforting her—insisting he didn't have any kind of diseases she would need to worry about, and if by some odd stroke of luck he got her pregnant, he'd do the right thing by her. Glancing across the room, he noticed Brandon had disappeared back inside the bathroom and shut the door. *Coward.*

He reached over, wrapping an arm around her shoulders and pulling her up against his side. "I should be comfortin' you. Not the other way around."

With her head resting on his chest and her fingers slipping through the hair scattered over his skin, he could almost lose himself in her and the odd notion of a future with her. He'd never thought about a future with a bed partner before, and the thought of having Emma for more than a few nights confused him.

"We all make mistakes, Beau. You're human, just like me."

"No, you're perfect." *How could Emma think she was anything, but ideal?* From everything he'd seen of her with her friends and family, she cared with her whole heart—taking on things most people would have let others deal with.

She propped herself up on her elbow and stared down at him. "Yeah—whatever. I'm not perfect. Not even close. I make mistakes all the time."

"Like what?"

Her bottom lip disappeared between her teeth, and he had the insane urge to bite it and pull it into his mouth.

"Well, even though I ride barrels during the rodeo events, I don't practice like I should."

He almost rolled his eyes, but he couldn't stop the small smile on his lips.

"I'm a terrible sister."

"How so?"

"I know my sister Elizabeth told someone about you and Brandon being out at our house. When I saw her this afternoon, I chewed her out for blabbing."

"I'm sure she's worried about you," he said, wondering why she wanted to hide their relationship. *Relationship? This isn't a relationship. It's a few fun filled nights with a hot woman.*

Emma slipped her fingers down his side and back up, and his body couldn't help but respond to the intimate touch.

"I know, but I didn't have to jump all over her for it." She glanced up and stared right into his eyes. "How many women have you and Brandon shared?"

I think my world narrowed to a small shaft of light I should be runnin' for to save my ass. The last thing she needs to know is how many women Brandon and I have shared.

"Um, I don't know. Why?" he croaked.

Most people looked stupid doing the one-shoulder shrug, but on Emma, it looked cute. Everything about her screamed 'keeper.' *No, not after only knowing her two days.*

"I'm curious, I guess. It's not like I do this sort of thing all the time," she replied, swirling her finger through his chest hair. "You two seem to have the whole thing down to a science." She sat up and pulled her knees to her chest. "I don't really know anything about you."

"Sure you do. You're a Brandon Tucker fan. Take all his information and multiple it times two."

"Not true, Beau. You two may look alike, but you're nothin' like him." Tucking a piece of hair behind her ear, she continued. "Tell me about Beau Tucker. Tell me the things you like to do, things *you* enjoy."

She can see that? No one's ever figured that out before.

"Okay. I don't know how much you know about Brandon outside of what the media gives you, so I'll start from the beginning." He scooted up and leaned back against the headboard. "I'm ten minutes older than Brandon. I guess you could say that's why I feel obligated to take care of him. Our parents own some ranch land up near Sun Prairie."

"Go on," she whispered, lying down next to him and putting her head on his chest again.

He loved having her this close, her breasts pressed against his side, the warmth of her skin scorching him like a branding iron.

"We did the cattle thing during high school and for a little while afterwards, but Brandon always had talent. He could sing the hell out of any country tune he heard, and he did. Rodeos, festivals, weddings—you name it, he sang at it. Then, one day, he got this bright idea to start playing in a couple of bars as their house band. A couple of his buddies played instruments, so they started up a band and got a few gigs around home. After a while, he branched out and started getting dates all over the country. One night, when he was doing a show in Nashville at one of the dive honky-tonks, a record guy came up to him after his show and told him he wanted to see him in his office the next day. Brandon almost blew the guy off."

"Seriously? He could have killed his career."

"Yeah. He told me about the guy later that night and I convinced him to go see him the next day. Brandon always wanted to be a country star, and now he is. I told him I'd be there with him, for however long the ride lasted."

"What about you? I'm sure you have dreams of your own."

Silence stretched between them for some time while he argued with himself about telling her his heart's desire. The words he'd refused to utter for the last six years hovered on the tip of his tongue. *Would it be safe to tell her and expose all my hopes and dreams—things I couldn't even share with Brandon earlier when he asked?*

"I…"

Brandon opened the bathroom door and said, "Are you two done shootin' the shit out here? I'm tired of hangin' out in the bathroom. I need some sleep if I'm going to keep up my energy for Emma's tutelage in threesomes."

"There *is* another bed, Brandon," she replied, glaring daggers at him. "Maybe Beau and I would like to talk for a while."

Brandon snorted. "Fine. I would have rather curled up behind you while I slept, but since you two seem to have this need to yak, I'll grab the other bed."

"He can be such an ass," she murmured.

"Yes, he can."

"As you were saying," she said, encouraging him to take up where their conversation had lagged when Brandon came out of the bathroom.

"It's not important. We should really get some sleep too." He circled her nipple with one finger, watching in fascination as it hardened.

"You keep doin' that and sleep is the last thing gonna happen."

"You'd have sex with me without Brandon here?"

Her eyes widened in shock. "Are you serious? Of course, I would. We pretty much did it without him here a little while ago—and I'm sure you know exactly how hot you are, so I don't have to tell you."

"Tell me anyway," he replied, wanting to hear her voice more than anything. The moment she'd screamed his name when she climaxed the first time, he'd wanted to hear it over and over.

She licked her lips and draped herself over his chest. "You have the most amazing eyes. Did I ever tell you how much I love brown eyes?"

"No."

"Well, I do. Yours remind me of milk chocolate. Smooth and appealing, with all the sweetness wrapped up inside them. And when they sparkle? Mmm. You could get me to do anythin' you want."

"Anythin'? Could get interesting. Go on."

"And you have a smile that could melt any woman's heart into a puddle."

"Yours?"

"Maybe." She shifted and slid her body down his chest, letting her nipples rub against every inch of him until she stopped with her mouth hovering over his nipple, stirring his cock to life.

"And your chest looks good enough to nibble on." She grazed her teeth over his left nipple. "Just the right amount of chest hair—and it's so soft, it tickles my breasts when I do this…"

He fought the groan in his chest as she lifted up so only her nipples slipped through his chest hair before moving up more and dangling them close to his mouth. If he moved toward her, he could capture one between his lips. *God! The woman could tempt Saint Peter himself—and being only a lowly mortal, I can't resist.*

"And your cock—did I talk about your cock yet?" she asked, sliding back down to straddle his hips.

"No," he whispered, his cock beginning to ache with the need to be inside her.

"When you were inside me, you filled me up so completely." Emma scooted back further and bent low over his cock. "Silk over a steel rod." She wrapped her hand around him and squeezed.

"Fuck, Emma. You're killin' me here, darlin'."

The wet slide of her tongue against his aching flesh about did him in. "You taste fantastic, Beau. A little salty, but not bitter or anything. I loved swallowing all of your cum. Wanna do it again?"

Torn between wanting her to suck him off or fuck her until she came, milking his cock for every drop of cum, he hesitated.

"Somethin' wrong?"

"God, no. I can't decide." Grabbing her under her arms, he pulled her up so she lay on top of him. "I want you, Emma."

"I want you too, Beau. The two of us together could light this bed on fire."

"What about Brandon?"

"I don't want Brandon right now. I want you and only you." With her knees up by his sides, his cock head brushed against her open and waiting pussy lips. "I need your cock. Every magnificent inch."

A fine layer of sweat coated his body as he fought the need rushing through him. Blood roared in his ears. His balls ached and his cock screamed for release.

"What's it gonna be boy?"

"Ride me, darlin'," he growled, pushing her hips down and shoving his cock deep inside her.

"Oh yeah. Perfect," she purred, widening her legs even further and giving him an inch or two more room.

She started to rock her hips, riding him like she would a wild stallion or an untamed bull at the rodeo. Her breasts bounced with each thrust of his hips, until he cradled them in both hands and let her take the reins of their ride. "So good."

"You're so fuckin' tight, Emma. Hot. Scorching hot. Burn me, baby."

Leaning on her hands, she thrust her breasts further into his palms, tossed her head back so her hair tickled his thighs, and squeezed her pussy muscles around him.

"Fuck me, Beau. God, yes. Cram that cock deep. Hit my sweet spot. You know where it is. You hit it earlier."

He pulled his feet up to brace himself on the bed and shoved his cock so deep the air rushed from her lungs on a moan.

"Right there. Hard. Oh yes, hard."

The bed banged against the wall as he shoved every inch of his cock into her squeezing, milking, burning pussy. When she climaxed, his name came from her mouth like a prayer and her pussy held him tight, refusing to let him go until he'd spilled every last drop of cum deep inside her scorching pussy.

"Sweet baby Jesus," he murmured, feeling like he'd shot every ounce of his energy out the end of his cock.

Emma crawled up beside and collapsed next to him on the bed. "Damn, you're good."

"Why thank you, ma'am."

With the last bit of energy he possessed, he curled an arm around her shoulder and pulled her next to him. Sleep tickled the edges of his consciousness even as she grabbed the sheet and pulled it up over them, curling into his embrace with a contented sigh.

"Night, Beau."

"Night, darlin'."

Chapter Seven

Morning light tickled her eyelids, spearing them with brightness and forcing Emma to open them. She groaned and rolled away, only to come up against a hard body. Shoving her hair out of her face, she sat up, holding the sheet to her breasts and staring at the man next to her. *Beau or Brandon?* Without cologne or a single visual clue, she couldn't tell the difference. The light coming through the windows wasn't much, and it made it hard to see.

Bits and pieces of the night before flashed across her mind, bringing with them the memory of Beau making love to her before they fell into exhausted sleep. Even without the slight difference in eye color to tell them apart, she knew Beau lay snoring softly next to her. Given a moment to study him, she propped herself up on her hand so she could let her gaze roam over his features, taking in everything about him. His hair looked so soft, reminding her of the ticklish brush of those locks against the skin of her thighs when he'd eaten her pussy until she screamed his name. It carried a wave, and her fingers itched to run through those silky strands.

She knew his brown eyes had gold flecks in them where Brandon's didn't, and right now, she longed to see them smiling at her with a little twinkle of mischief. The slope of his nose looked regal and straight except for a bump at the bridge where he'd broken it at some point. She frowned, hoping her impromptu head-butt the night before hadn't caused any permanent damage. A bruise had formed near the bridge, but nothing giving her any indication she'd broken it again, thank goodness.

The width of his shoulders and the muscles of his chest displayed strong, work toughened power where the sheet had slipped down his body, and she wondered what he did besides take care of things for Brandon to have such an exceptional physique. The sheet covered his hips, cock and legs, but her memory brought into sharp clarity the length and thickness of his impressive shaft and the firmness with which he'd taken control of their lovemaking the night before.

"Do I meet with your mornin' approval, darlin'?"

Her gaze ricocheted back to his face and heat flushed her cheeks. The appreciation in his gaze warmed her whole body, and she relaxed back against the sheets as they switched positions and he loomed over her.

"My turn," he whispered, slowly pulling the sheet down to expose her breasts. "Mmm. Nice." He licked his finger and circled her left nipple until it stood up, hard and begging for his touch. "You have beautiful skin. So soft and smooth. I love touching you."

Her nipple ached for the heat of mouth against it. Unable to stop, she shoved her breast further into his touch and whimpered low in her throat when the warm wetness closed over the tip. Continuing to pull the sheet down, he exposed first her belly button ring and then the springy curls guarding her pussy. The brush of his lips as he worked his way down tickled her skin, causing it to quiver and jump.

He dipped his tongue into her belly button, flicking the jewel dangling there. "I love these things. They are so damned sexy."

The moment his hand slipped through the curls and skimmed over her clit, her whole body shuddered. She spread her thighs, begging in a whisper, wanting his hands, his mouth, his cock—something to fill the empty void. With her eyes closed, every sensation, every touch brought her desire to an explosive level. The calluses on his hands felt rough and erotic, scraping over her sensitive skin. His fingers left her pussy, and his mouth moved back up to her breast to suck and nip at the tip.

Her eyes flew open when, seconds later, she felt the wet slide of a tongue over her clit.

Brandon winked from between her spread thighs. "Mornin', honey. Wakin' up like this…mmm…a man could get used to it real easy."

Beau's moist mouth moved from her breast to say, "Are you up for ridin' double this mornin', darlin'?"

Ridin' double? Are they serious?

"You mean—"

"One of us in your ass and the other in your pussy," Beau explained, still circling her nipple with his finger.

Her heart hammered, and her ears rang. Just the thought of having both of them at once flushed her body with desire so strong, it made her shiver.

"Don't worry, Emma. We'll make sure you're good and ready before anythin' happens, and if you don't like it, we'll stop. We don't want to hurt you."

Staring into Beau's eyes, she knew he spoke the truth. No matter what, he wouldn't allow her to be hurt. The small nod of her head gave them the answer they sought.

Brandon's wicked tongue danced over her clit, flicking and circling until it throbbed with the beat of her heart. When he slipped two fingers into her pussy, she spread her thighs more and moaned into Beau's mouth as he took possession of her lips. Having two men focused on her needs seemed almost selfish, but with Brandon between her legs and Beau eating at her mouth, she relaxed and let them do whatever they wanted.

The tip of a finger gathered some of her juices and then probed at her back hole, making her stiffen again.

"Easy, honey," Brandon purred, pushing it through the grasping muscles of her anus.

She hissed at the small burn, but it soon turned into a different type of pleasure as he added another finger, stretching her by scissoring those tempting digits. The unmistakable urge to press back against his hand overwhelmed her and tore a moan from deep inside, only to be swallowed up by Beau's mouth. Brandon finger fucked both holes and ate at her clit, sucking it into his mouth until her whole body hummed and quivered. Both her legs trembled as she clung to the edge of climax by her fingernails, trying to get to the other side, but not having quite the right sensation. Beau had relinquished her mouth for her breast, flicking and circling the nipple until it stood up, begging for him to suck until it turned a bright rosy red.

A high keen exploded from her lips when her climax crashed through her, stealing her breath and making her heart hammer so hard she thought it would burst through her chest. Her men continued their assault on her senses until she exploded into a second climax before the first one even finished.

"Think she's ready?" Brandon asked, pulling himself up to sit between her thighs.

"More than ready." Beau tossed him a condom and slipped one on himself before he pulled the tube of lube from the nightstand drawer and laid it on the bed. "Okay, darlin'. This is what we're gonna do." He slipped one arm around her and hauled her over his chest so she straddled his waist. "Open your hot little pussy for me."

The nudge of his cock at her opening awakened all the nerve endings in her pussy again as he slowly entered her body. A soft moan escaped her lips, and she leaned into him. With both hands on her hips, he pushed her down onto his cock, impaling her clear to the root.

"God, you're so tight, Emma. It's gonna be even tighter with Brandon in your ass."

She'd almost forgotten Brandon kneeling behind her until he nudged at her back hole. Beau reached up and flipped him the tube of lube. The next thing she felt was the cold smear of wet lubrication on her asshole. Brandon pushed some into her hole and massaged it around her in passage with his fingers.

"Relax, honey."

Beau shifted and eased his cock in and out of her pussy in shallow, slow strokes, while Brandon slicked her up and then bumped the head of his dick against her. She sucked in a ragged breath as the full head speared through her sphincter in a small pop.

"Goddamn, you're tight," Brandon hissed.

She could feel his hands trembling where they gripped her hips as he fought not to fuck her hard. God love both of them. The initial burn of his penetration eased into the most amazing feeling. Her pussy thrummed and spasmed with each inch of Brandon's cock easing into her hole and stretching her until she felt completely full.

"You okay, darlin'?" Beau asked as his lips brushed her hair.

"Yeah. Incredible."

"Fuck, yeah," Brandon replied.

A small wiggle of her hips brought a hiss from both men—her men...for tonight anyway. "You need to move. Both of you. Now."

With practiced ease, the two of them fell into a steady alternating rhythm, Beau penetrating her pussy and Brandon's dick in her ass. A whimper escaped her lip and her whole body trembled with the need to come, but something held her off. She grasped at the motions of their bodies, hoping she could pluck the elusive climax from the air.

"Somethin's not right, Brandon." They both stopped, and tears burned her eyelids.

"God, please don't stop," Emma whimpered.

"Tell me what to do, baby," Beau whispered, kissing her eyelids.

"My clit. Rub it."

His hand snaked down between their bodies, swirled through the lubrication caused by their joining, and rasped over her clit. At first his touch was soft, until she whimpered and moved her hips. Both men began to fuck her in earnest, and Beau's finger pressed hard against her clit, doing a little figure eight move and then flicking it back and forth.

Her high pitched scream of release bounced off the walls of the room. "Oh God!"

Several moments later, she collapsed on Beau's chest, but the pounding of their hips never lessened.

Desire speared through her again, and she huffed an exhausted burst of air over the sweaty skin beneath her cheek. A smaller climax rushed through her, holding her body in its grasp. Within seconds Brandon growled his release behind her, and then Beau groaned as his climax hit him too.

The three of them stayed together, locked in passionate embrace, until Emma heard her cell phone ring. "Shit! Move!"

"What the hell?" Brandon grumbled, sliding his soft cock from her ass.

"Emma?" Beau asked.

"It's my dad. If I don't answer it, he'll freak!" She scrambled from the bed, grabbed her pants from the floor, and flipped open her phone with a winded 'hello.'

"Emma? Where are you honey? You didn't come home last night."

The question made her spin around and hush the two men in the room with her. "I'm fine, Dad. I spent the night with Becky."

"Oh really?"

"Yeah. We helped Seth set up the beer tent and stuff last night. It was late when we left so I just crashed at her place. No biggie."

"Mmm. Want to tell me why you're lying to me, daughter?"

"But Daddy, I'm not—"

"Emma Leanne Weston. Don't you dare lie to me again. Becky called this morning looking for you, so I know you did spend the night at her house. Now where are you?"

"I'm sorry." She chewed her bottom lip and glanced at Beau and Brandon. "I'm at the hotel in town."

"Why?"

"I stayed with Beau and Brandon last night."

"Excuse me? I thought you weren't even talking to those two after you kicked them out of our house the other night."

"I know, but things changed, and I spent the night here."

"I'm sad you felt the need to lie to me, Emma, but I'm not going to lecture you. I just hope you aren't getting into somethin' that will hurt you in the end."

The disappointment in his voice tore at her heart. "But Daddy…"

"I'll see you when you get home, Emma." The silence had her biting her lip. "No matter what, sweetie, I love you."

"Thanks Dad. I love you too," she choked out as the phone clicked in her ear. "God, I'm so stupid!"

"Emma," Beau whispered in her ear, wrapping his arms around her. "You aren't stupid, darlin'. You have needs."

She quickly stepped out of his embrace and spun around. "Needs that can't be satisfied by one man, Beau? This kind of thing isn't normal. I heard the talk around town when Natalie, Cade, and Kale were dating. It was ugly. Do you think I want people to talk about me like that?"

"Honey, no one has to know what happens between the three of us. Beau and I wouldn't talk," Brandon said, stopping next to Beau.

"It doesn't matter. People saw me come in here with you two. I'd be surprised if the whole fuckin' town isn't talkin' already." She crumpled into the chair in the corner and dropped her face into her hands. "What the hell was I thinkin?" A moment later she jumped to her feet and grabbed her clothes from the floor, pulling them on. "I wasn't. The whole thing was impetuous. My mom always said I didn't think things through. Boy, was she right."

"Emma, wait," Beau said, pulling on his own clothes. "Don't leave like this."

"Like what, Beau? This whole thing was a huge mistake. I can't keep one man satisfied, much less two. And you two?" She shook her head and grabbed her keys. "Look at you. Either of you could have whoever you want. I'm a girl from a dinky town in the middle of nowhere, Montana. I couldn't hang onto a man for any length of time if I tried. I'm too tomboy. I've got a big mouth, and I talk tough. Men don't like those traits in a woman. I'm not sophisticated. I'm not beautiful."

"Don't insult yourself, Emma," Brandon said, grabbing her hand and pulling her down on the edge of the bed before she could make her escape. "You're a beautiful woman."

"I hate when people patronize me, Brandon, so please don't."

"I'm not. You are beautiful and sexy." His finger traced along her cheek.

"I need to go," she whispered, not really wanting to leave. Her head warred with her heart.

"Stay."

"No." She jumped to her feet and headed for the door. "Thanks for a good time, guys." After a quick glance behind her, she left without another word.

* * * *

"What the hell just happened?" Beau growled, running his hands through his hair. "Everything was going great."

"I know, Beau," Brandon replied, mimicking his brother's frustrated gesture as he watched the door slam behind Emma's departure. "We'll talk to her again later, at the rodeo. Maybe she'll be ready to listen there."

"Yeah—with a thousand people around, including her family? Are you nuts?"

"Maybe, but I know one thing. I'm not done with little Miss Emma Weston. Not by a long shot." He got to his feet and headed for the bathroom. "I'm taking a shower, and then you can have the bathroom if you want. We need to make sure everything is set for the show this evening anyway. We've got some work to do. I want to be out there around the people today. The more I can interact with them, the more we'll have at the show, and the more money we'll make for Charlene."

"All right. I'll make some phone calls while you're in the shower. We'll need to stop at the garage so we can get your amps off the bus and some of the light setups out of the trailer."

After a quick shower, Brandon picked out the standard cowboy attire. *Damn, I haven't worn the whole outfit in a while.* Fastening each snap on the front and at his wrists, he thought of Emma. Would she be the type to love flinging those snaps open with a quick tug? His cock hardened behind the fly of his jeans just thinking about her. Being inside her ass earlier was heaven. He'd never felt anyone so tight and so perfect. Double penetration with her wasn't like anything he'd experienced before, and he and Beau had done it with a few. Her whimpers, moans, and ultimately her scream of climax had burned through his balls and made him ache to have her again. *Enough. You don't need any kind of entanglements, no matter how enticing the woman.*

Brandon returned to the living room area of the suite, where Beau sat on the couch with a pad of paper on his lap and his phone to his ear.

"Hey, Brandon. I've got things situated. Are you planning on hanging out by the bleachers and around the concession stands? Do we need to alert the local police for security?" Beau asked, shutting his phone and laying it on the table.

"It probably wouldn't be a bad idea to have a couple of cops on standby in case. I don't think it'll be a big deal once the announcement is made why we're doing this." He glanced at his brother and cocked his head to the side. "Are you gonna ride?"

Beau ran his hand over his stubbled cheek and jaw. "I think so. If I win, I can donate the money to Charlene."

"You haven't ridden bulls in a while, Beau. I don't want you gettin' hurt."

"I'll be fine. It hasn't been more than a year or so."

"Since when?" He sometimes forgot Beau had a life outside of the one they had together, but it shocked him to think his brother had ridden bulls while he'd been busy elsewhere.

"I hit a couple of rodeos last year when you went on vacation to the Bahamas with Anita."

Brandon thought back to mistake upon mistake with Anita. He'd thought himself in love with her, until he'd realized she'd liked the fame and recognition of being Brandon Tucker's woman—not him. Sex between them was hot at first, but when he'd started getting into a little kink with her—nothing major, just swatting her butt, wanting to tie her hands to the headboard so he could eat her out until she couldn't move, those kinds of things—she'd absolutely refused to discuss it. He'd even thought about marrying her at one time. Thank God he'd come to his senses without asking. Manipulation came naturally to her, but once he'd realized what she really wanted, he'd dumped her like a hot rock.

No woman could hold his attention long enough even to think about permanent anymore—well, maybe one, and he didn't know whether anything might come of this intoxicating attraction to her. "Well, just make sure you wear your vest and helmet. I don't need you ending up in the hospital."

"Worried about me, brother, or just worried no one else will be able to keep you out of trouble?"

"We fight. Brothers do those kinds of things, Beau, but you know you mean everything to me. If I didn't have you, I'd lose my mind and probably drown myself in a bottle." He laid a hand on Beau's shoulder. "If I haven't told you lately how much I appreciate all you do for me, then I've been an ass."

"You *are* an ass, Brandon. I don't think you've uttered *thank you* since this whole party began."

Brandon frowned and thought about that. He hadn't ever said thank you, and looking back now, he realized just how badly he'd acted the spoiled country star. Everything was about what Brandon wanted, and Beau always made it happen for him, but he'd never understood the sacrifices Beau made to be by his side. The whole idea felt like a punch to the gut. "I'm sorry. I've come to realize in the several days or so, I've been completely selfish, taking up your time and energy to keep everything running for me. You gave up all your dreams, and I don't know how I'd be able to handle this whole star thing without you."

Beau shot him a thoughtful look and said, "Fine. I need a raise."

"A raise?"

"Yep."

"How can you get a raise from nothin'?" Brandon asked with a chuckle.

"You'd be surprised how much you pay me, brother."

"Maybe I need to take a better look at my finances."

"Maybe you do, but trust me, I haven't done anything illegal or unethical. You also donate to several charities, by the way, and you're still a very rich man. You couldn't spend all your money in this lifetime."

He glanced at his brother, realizing he really had no clue how much money he had or where even a third of it might be located. When he needed money, Beau made sure he had it. Beau kept the accounting, booked his shows, made sure he got there on time, and kept him out of trouble. About the only thing Beau didn't do was screw his women for him, but since they shared Emma, he couldn't even say that. What a wakeup call this trip into small-town Montana had been. It was time for Brandon Tucker to take his life and his career into his own hands.

"We'll talk about this more, Beau. Right now, we need to get the equipment and get out to the fairgrounds. If we want to corner Emma, we need to make sure we keep a good eye on her."

"Yes, we do. I'll be out in a minute," Beau replied, heading for the bathroom.

Brandon walked to the window and stared out at the people moving up and down the sidewalk and the trucks zipping past on their way to God only knew where, while he waited for Beau to get ready. All this thinking about how Beau handled everything had gotten him to realize he didn't have any say in what he did anymore. He needed to take more control over his own life. He loved Beau, but his brother needed to follow his own dreams for a change, and he knew Beau's dreams included bull riding, even if the stubborn asshole got himself killed.

Chapter Eight

The crowd in the stands and milling around the fairgrounds always amazed Emma. People came in from miles around to attend the Founder's Day events—the rodeo, the picnic on Sunday, and the fireworks display at the end of the weekend over the lake. Usually, she mingled with her friends, hung out with some of the cowboys, served beer in the tent for Seth, and flirted here and there. Cowboys of every creed and color lined up for their shot at bull riding, calf roping, steer wrestling, and picking up the ladies. Stetson, Resistol, and straw hats adorned every cowboy and most cowgirls as they moved in and out of the crowd, talking, laughing, and making new friends.

She hadn't seen Beau or Brandon since she arrived, and she hoped she didn't. Staying away from those two would be her best choice, since fallin' into bed with them had turned into a mistake—a mistake because her heart seemed drawn to the two men, even when her head said the whole situation was wrong. The chance of running into one or both kept her from doing too much mingling. If she could avoid them for the rest of the weekend, she might make it out of this predicament without making a fool of herself.

Right after her event, Emma rode straight for the livestock barn to put her horse away. The last place she figured she'd run into either of the Tucker boys would be in the stable and it gave her a few minutes to think.

She'd only known them a few days, never mind the five years of following Brandon's career and eking out every bit of information on him she could find. She must keep herself separated from the temptation the two of them placed in front of her. *I'll just have to avoid them.* Once she finished brushing her horse, she walked him into his stall and locked the door. She took a deep breath and shored up her resolve before she headed for the beer tent.

A deep, sexy laugh floated to her on the breeze and made her turn toward the sound, goose bumps pimpling the skin of her arms. She knew the sound—she'd heard it a few times last night along with the whispers, groans, whimpers, and sighs of satisfied lovers. *Damn it!* Sure enough, Brandon Tucker stood surrounded by five women near the bottom steps of the spectator stands. Each girl took turns taking pictures with him, wrapping her arms around him and hugging him so tight you couldn't squeeze a piece of newspaper between their bodies. Jealousy burned in Emma's gut. *I have no right to be jealous. He's not mine.* Her head warred with her heart. She wanted to tear each of those women away from his side and plaster herself between him and Beau.

Unable to stop herself from drifting closer, she moved around the back of the stands. From here, she could hear and see everything going on, even though she wanted to kick her own ass for caring.

"Well now, honey. I'd love to dance with you later. I have a show to do first, and then I'll be free. We're raisin' money for Charlene at the concert, so make sure you're real generous."

Damn that Betty Carter. The slut.

"I'm sure I could show you a real good time, Brandon. I've been in love with your singin' since I first heard you."

"Thank you. You know, I sing every song to a beautiful woman durin' a show?"

"Really? I'd love for you to sing to me."

"I'll see what I can do, honey. Just make sure you leave some money in the collection barrel for Charlene, and I'll sing one just for you."

"Done deal, Brandon." Betty locked her lips with his, and he sure didn't look like he minded as he put his hands on her waist.

"Bastard," Emma grumbled quietly.

Once the kiss finally ended, the five women walked away—but not without wiggling their fingers at him and blowing kisses.

"You know I sing to a beautiful woman during a show?" Emma mimicked in a singsong voice. "Yeah, and you sleep with whoever you can get to drop her underwear."

"Jealous, darlin'?" Beau whispered next to her ear.

She squeaked as she jumped back, banging her head on a low bar on the stands. "Ouch!"

"Serves you right for eavesdroppin', Emma." His warm hand rubbed the spot on her head.

"I wasn't eavesdroppin', and why did you sneak up on me?"

"You've been avoidin' me and Brandon all afternoon, and when I saw you over here watchin' Brandon with those girls, I wanted to corner you."

"Why?"

"For this." He grabbed her around the waist and pulled her to him, his intent clear in his eyes. The brush of his lips against hers made need shoot straight to her pussy. How he managed to crank her up so damned fast, she didn't know—and right now, she didn't care. Having his lips on hers brought back every feeling, every thought, and every raunchy thing they did last night and this morning as vivid pictures in her mind.

After he'd kissed her thoroughly, she sighed and opened her eyes.

"There's a look worth findin', darlin'."

Brandon came around the edge of the bleachers and stopped next to them. "Caught her listenin', Beau?"

"Yep, and she wasn't too happy with your little scene, brother."

"I didn't figure she would be. Why'd you think I did it?"

"Wait, what? You knew I was back here?" She spun around and stepped away, jamming her fists on her hips and then tapping her boot on the hard dirt.

Brandon slipped one fingertip down her cheek, and she could feel her traitorous nipples bead into hard nubs.

"Of course, honey." The finger moved to skim over her bottom lip. "Otherwise, I wouldn't have let that woman kiss me."

The smirk on his sexy lips made her want to smack him and lick him all over at the same time. "I... Damn it!"

"Nothin' to be jealous of, honey."

Beau slipped his arm back around her waist, tugging her to his side. "Brandon is makin' the rounds, darlin'."

"I see that, Beau. Apparently, he's makin' the rounds with several willin' women."

"I didn't mean it like that," Beau said.

"I have to mingle with the crowd, Emma. We need them to be at the show and drop lots of cash in the barrel for Charlene. The more I move in and out of the crowd, huggin', kissin', and shakin' hands, the more money they'll drop during my performance."

The logic of their words hit her like a ton of bricks. "You mean you didn't want to kiss her?"

Brandon moved in close enough she could feel the warmth of his breath on her lips and see the heat of desire in his eyes. "The only woman I want to kiss is you. To feel your soft lips under mine. To slip my tongue between them and tangle it with yours until we're both breathin' hard."

Sandwiched between the two of them like this, her heart and her mind went spinning out of control with need so strong she moaned. Her body betrayed her to both men, and she could see the understanding pass between them when their eyes met.

Brandon licked her lips slowly, and she moaned and closed her eyes.

The need spiraling through her scared her—this wasn't like her at all. What kind of power did these two devastatingly handsome cowboys hold? How did they make her forget everything but the heat of their bodies around her?

"You'll meet us later?" Beau whispered, the tip of his tongue teasing her earlobe. "After the show and everything is over with?"

"Yes," she murmured, unable to stay away from their intoxicating presence.

"I can't wait to see you spread out on the bed again, Emma, breasts begging for the wetness of a tongue, pussy dripping with cream and glistening in the soft lamp light as your body quivers with desire," Beau continued, while Brandon teased her nipple with his finger.

How the hell he'd gotten under her shirt without her realizing it, she didn't know, but the calluses on his fingers played hell with her need. A quick glance over his shoulder confirmed the two men blocked anyone else from seeing what they were doing to her.

"I—I have to go," she stammered, backing up and pushing her shirt back into the waistband of her jeans.

She sidestepped away from them, sighing heavily. *Get a fuckin' grip, Emma. Jesus.* A look over her shoulder showed her twin bulges in their jeans and sexy grins on their lips.

* * * *

The masses coming into the beer tent blew her mind. Where in hell did all these people come from? She didn't know, but her feet were killing her. "Hey, Seth, I need a break."

"Sure, Emma. Go get some air. I hear the bullridin' is starting soon, and I know how much you like to watch it."

"Thanks," she replied, giving him a small smile. He really was a nice guy.

Warm air hit her like a furnace blast when she stepped outside the tent. Sweat trickled down between her breasts, tickling her skin, but she paid it no mind. She needed to get her mind off Brandon and Beau. For the last two hours, they'd been in and out of the beer tent several times. Once or twice with women on their arms, and sometimes alone, but they always managed to get in her line for their beers. Her jaw hurt from grinding her teeth together while they paraded women through the tent. They'd said it helped with the charity event. She wasn't so sure.

Emma heard the announcer begin his speech. "Welcome, ladies and gentlemen, to this year's Founder's Day Rodeo."

The crowd let out a huge cheer.

"Unlike previous years where the bull-riding came last, we are going to run a few riders through on the bulls first, since we have so many contestants. After the first five riders have gone, we'll move onto some calf-ropin', barrel racin', steer wrestlin', and some kids' events. So hang onto your hats, folks—grab a beer and pull up a seat, 'cause we've got a show for you."

Emma made her way toward the split rail fencing and climbed up on the bottom rung. The bull chute stood on the far end of the circular arena from where she took up a spot, but she'd have a good view once the ride began.

"One more thing, folks. We are pleased to let you all know one of country music's hottest talents is spendin' a few days with us here in Red Rock, and he's graciously donated his time to put on a benefit show this evening for our own Charlene Campbell. Brandon Tucker will be putting on an acoustic show at three in the beer tent. Now, folks, admission is free, but we do expect everyone to drop a few bucks in the barrel we'll have near the door. Give generously—this is to help Charlene parents with her monstrous hospital bills."

Another loud cheer went up, with a few feet stomping in the stands. Emma smiled. Brandon's generosity amazed her. A free concert would bring in tons of cash, she hoped.

Three riders did their turns on the bull, two of them missing the buzzer by at least a second or two. The bulls seemed unnaturally ornery today—or it seemed that way to her anyway. Dust swirled in the air, coating everything within twenty feet of the railing with a thin layer, including her.

She hopped down and brushed the dirt from her jeans and shirt until the announcer's words penetrated her brain, chilling her to the bone.

"Next up is… Wow. Folks, this is a special treat. Right now, we have Beau Tucker, former top ten ranked rider, up to try his luck on the bulls. Now, Beau's been ridin' off and on for a few years, but this is the first time he's been on a bull in over a year. Give it up for Beau Tucker, ladies and gentlemen. Beau has also said he will donate any winnin's to Charlene's folks."

Emma spun around with her heart in her throat. She watched the chute spring open, and the biggest, scariest bull she'd ever seen whipped Beau around like a rag doll. His arm, lifted high and to the right, waved back and forth with each twist and turn the bull tried. The muscles of his back bunched and rolled, and his biceps rippled as he held onto the bull-rope and concentrated on staying on the huge animal.

"Come on Beau. Come on," she whispered, almost as a mantra, her eyes glued to his body. If he got hurt, she wouldn't be able to handle it. She'd seen dozens of men hurt riding bulls, but this was Beau! One of the men who'd wormed their way into her heart, whether she wanted him to or not, and damn it, she had plans for this evening that included him buck-assed naked and not broken into painful pieces. Time seemed to stand still. Her fingers gripped the rail beneath her until her nails dug into the wood. The clock slowly ticked off eight seconds, and he stayed on the bull. When the buzzer sounded, he unwrapped his hand and jumped clear before racing for the railing right in front of her.

"Are you fuckin' crazy?" she yelled as he vaulted over the rail and landed at her feet. "You could have been killed, Beau."

A sexy grin flashed across his face, and he bent down and kissed her soundly on the mouth. "I didn't know you cared, darlin'."

"Of course I care. Damn it!"

"Easy, Emma. I've done this before. Piece of cake. That bull wasn't even tryin' hard."

"You really are crazy," she snapped, and spun on her heels to return to the beer tent.

"Emma, wait," he said, grabbing her elbow and spinning her around to face him. "I'm fine." He brushed his hands over his jeans, patted his chest where the safety vest encased his body and stomped his feet to prove he hadn't been hurt. "See. Nothin' broken, nothin' bruised. All in one piece."

"This time. What about next time? What happens when one of those crazy animals throws you off and charges you? Huh? Then what, Beau?"

"It's not a big deal, Emma."

"Yes it is!"

"What's goin' on over here?" Brandon asked, stopping at her side.

"And you!" She poked her finger into the middle of Brandon's chest.

"Ouch."

"How in the hell can you let him ride bulls? Are you crazy, too?"

"Whoa, what brought this on?"

"She got a little hysterical when she saw me ride," Beau answered, crossing his arms over his chest.

"You had a good ride. Eight seconds and all."

"I am not hysterical." She paced back and forth for a moment and then faced them. "You know what? Fuck you. Both of you. Do whatever the hell you want to do. I don't care. Not a whit. Do you hear me? Not one little bit!"

With agitated steps, she headed back to the beer tent. Anger raced through her, but by the time she stepped behind the taps again, she wasn't sure what the hell she was angry about. She glanced at the growing crowd and sighed. Most of the patrons were still out in the stands watching the events, giving her a few moments to contemplate what had just happened out there between her, Beau, and Brandon, but not many. The tent would be overflowing soon. Yes, Beau could have gotten killed, but didn't the announcer say he'd been doing this for a while? Blowing up in front of both of them probably wasn't the smartest thing she could have done. Hell, it probably told them how much she cared, even though she'd spouted off that she didn't.

"You okay?" Becky asked as she poured another beer. "You look upset."

"I'm fine," she snapped at her friend, and then murmured a quick, "Sorry."

"I heard them announce Beau was riding. How did he do?"

"You know, I don't even know. I jumped all in his shit about ridin', I didn't even look at his score."

Becky shook her head and grabbed another cup.

"What?"

"You are in so deep, you don't know which way is up. I hope you don't get your heart broken."

"Am not."

"Yes you are, Emma. Those two are so deep in your heart already, and you're upset because one of them could have been hurt. What does that tell you?"

Emma pulled her bottom lip between her teeth and bit down until it hurt. "What am I gonna do, Becky? They'll be gone soon, and I'll probably never see either of them again."

"Do you want both of them? And I mean *want* as in a forever kind of thing."

"I've known them all of a couple of days. How can I know?"

"Seriously? You've been a Brandon Tucker groupie for the last five years. You know the man's shoe size, his brand of shampoo, and whether he wears boxers or briefs. The only thing I'm not sure whether you've figured out yet is whether he lays his cock to the left or right."

"Size twelve, Axe shampoo, boxers, and he's a lefty."

"See?"

"It doesn't matter, Becky. Those are facts, nothing more. I bet every hardcore fan knows them."

Becky's eyebrow met her hairline as she gave Emma an I-don't-believe-you-said-that look. "You can't be serious."

"Well, I only recently figured out the boxers thing and which side his cock lays on." She glanced left and right before she dropped her voice low and said, "By the way, they're both hung."

"And you would know this how?"

Emma squeezed her eyes shut and grimaced. *Fucking big mouth.*

"You slept with them, didn't you? Both of them."

"Yes."

"Damn," Becky whispered. "Brave girl." Becky glanced around and then dropped her voice further. "How was it?"

"Becky!"

"What? Not like half the women around here haven't fantasized about having two men at once. I mean when all the talk of Natalie, Cade, and Kale flew from mouth to ear, I know I thought about it. Not that I would try it, but you know."

"Promise not to say anything."

"Cross my heart."

She spun them both so their backs were to taps and said, "I want it again and again. Having both cocks—"

"You didn't?"

"We did."

"Wow," Becky whispered.

The crowd started cheering when Brandon came through the tent flap and headed for the stage. Was it time for the show already? She glanced at her watch, and sure enough, almost three.

Once he hit the stage, he plugged in his guitar and pulled up the stool they'd set up. He calmed the crowd with a smile and a wave. Beau stood off to the side to watch and make sure the equipment didn't malfunction, and to possibly adjust sound levels during the show.

"Afternoon folks."

Another loud cheer.

"Where's my girl, Charlene?" He glanced to the left of the stage, where Charlene sat in a special chair next to her parents. Chemotherapy had caused her to lose most of her pretty brown hair, so she wore a cute pink hat with white pokadots, a white blouse, pink jeans, and matching pink cowboy boots. "Ah, there she is. Welcome, darlin'. This is for you and your parents for everything you've gone through and all you still have to endure. You see, I haven't been in your shoes bein' sick and all, but my brother and I lost a baby sister a long time ago to cancer. She only lived to the age of six, and I know I speak for both of us when I say we miss her every day."

You could have heard a pin drop in the dirt while the crowd absorbed Brandon's words and Emma almost cried for him. Her throat burned, and she swallowed, fighting the tears. This tidbit of information was probably the one thing she hadn't known about Brandon—well, other than having an identical twin. That little tidbit of information never leaked out either.

"So, let's get this party started, shall we? We're here to raise some serious cash for these folks. Loosen up those wallets and purses, ladies and gents, while I sit here and do a few songs for you."

For the next hour, Brandon sang almost every song he'd ever put out to radio and a few they hadn't released as singles. Emma sang along and danced behind the beer taps. Every once in a while she'd glance at Beau, and he'd smile and give her a sexy wink.

The crowds enjoyed the show immensely, if she could judge at all. Several people danced together at the back of the tent, and more clapped and sang along to the songs they knew.

"Last song, folks."

The crowd groaned and Brandon laughed. "I'd love to sit up here all night and play for y'all, but my fingers haven't played this much in a long time. I do want to do one more song for you. It's a ballad and one of my favorites, so grab yourself a pretty gal, couple up, and sway to the music."

Emma held her breath. His fingers plucked the first few chords of the song, and her heart tripped over itself when he started singing "The Love of My Life."

The soft brush of fingers on her arm brought her attention around, and she came face-to-face with Beau. "Will you dance with me, Emma?"

The only answer she could give was the small nod of her head.

Beau wrapped one arm around her waist, taking her right palm in his left as he tugged her close. "I've been dreamin' about holding you like this from the moment I saw you," he murmured into her ear.

Shivers rolled down her spine, and the hair on her arms stood up. She had Brandon Tucker singing her favorite song and his twin holding her close—dreams didn't come close to this moment. Well, maybe one. Making love last night to both of them outshone any dream she could have thought up. The reality of making love with Beau and Brandon couldn't have been more perfect.

As the last chords of the song drifted off into the night, silence filled the tent for a few seconds. Ear-splitting cheers, shouts, and clapping broke the quiet, and the crowd went wild. Emma broke the embrace and turned to watch Brandon step off the stage. Charlene had tears running down her cheeks when he stopped in front of her, gave her a kiss, and handed her his guitar.

"He gave her his guitar?" she murmured.

"Yeah. He figured since she was a fan, it would mean a lot to her," Beau answered in a low voice.

"Wow. I'm sure she's thrilled." *This whole situation makes Brandon the kind of guy I've always hoped he would be in person. Kind, caring, considerate, although he's arrogant and selfish sometimes, too.* "I should get back to the taps. Thanks for the dance, Beau."

"You're welcome, darlin'. I love holdin' you. I hope I get a chance to do it again." He gave her a small smile before walking back to his brother's side.

"Can I get a beer please?"

Emma spun around to meet the gaze of the one man she wished would disappear, Joshua Spence.

Chapter Nine

Joshua was a player. He liked his money, he liked his booze, and he figured any woman in the country would drop her underwear and spread her thighs for him if he asked. Emma hadn't been any different in the beginning. His blond hair, blue eyes, lithe body, and hard muscles turned several heads whenever he walked into a room, but his heart belonged to one person and one alone—himself. Joshua Spence was in love with himself. Arrogant, conceited, mean, and selfish, he'd never quite understood why Emma broke off their engagement.

"Well, well. If it isn't Miss Emma. How are ya doin', darlin'? I ain't seen you in a while."

"Josh." She rolled her eyes and grimaced. "What can I get you?"

"Besides you?" he asked, in his usual snarky tone.

She really did hate the man. "I'm not on the menu. Regular or light beer?"

"Come on, Emma. We had some good times together."

"Yeah, until I caught you with Betty while we were engaged."

Josh shrugged his shoulders and smiled like he hadn't done a thing wrong. "It was a mistake, and I've tried explainin' it to you, but you wouldn't listen."

"Nothin' to explain. You cheated, and I don't like cheaters. Get a life, Josh. I've moved on. You should, too."

"Moved on with who?"

His tone told her his own green-eyed monster had reared its ugly head, and she debated whether to tell him the truth or blow him off. "None of your business. You lost the ability to tell me what to do when I took off your ring and threw it at you."

"It's those two out-of-towners? The country guy and his brother? I saw you with them behind the stands." Josh's lips had pulled back into almost a snarl, giving Emma a little satisfaction that he'd seen her with Beau and Brandon. "When did you turn into such a slut—or did Cade rub off on you? You know, fuckin' his wife and his best friend and all."

Fury made her see red. The crack of her hand against his cheek echoed in a room gone suddenly silent at his words.

"What I do is none of your fuckin' business, Josh, and if you say one more word about Cade, Natalie, or Kale, you'll find out just what a bitch I can be." Rage raced down her back at his audacity. "And if I did fuck both Brandon and Beau, it's between the three of us." The sharp inhalation of air brought her attention to her dad standing off in the corner of the tent. "Shit." She glanced back at Josh and said, "Go find Betty. I'm sure she's free, since Brandon turned her down flat."

She walked to her dad's side and said, "Daddy, let me explain." Grasping his hand, she led him out behind the tent where they could talk in semi-privacy.

"You know how badly the town talked after what Cade did came out," her father said, once they'd stopped their hurried rush out of the beer tent.

"I know, Dad, but listen. This is different."

"How so, Emma? Did you or did you not sleep with those two men?" The disillusionment in his eyes broke her heart.

"Yes, I did, and if they'll have me, I plan to do it again. I care about them."

"You've only known them a few days."

"I know, but they've come to mean a lot to me in a short time. Will this work into something more permanent? I don't know, but I want to hold onto what we have—even if it's only for a few days."

A sigh of resignation left his mouth as he asked, "Are you sure?"

"Daddy, I'm twenty-four years old, and I know what I want."

"All grown up, huh," he said, brushing her hair back off her cheek and tucking the strands behind her ear.

"Sometimes you act like I'm still twelve," she said, sadness lacing her words. "I'm a woman, even though you seem to want me to stay a child."

He pulled her into a hug and then let her retreat a few inches. "I wish you would, Emma. You're my youngest. I hate to see you growing up so fast and furious, and I'm terrified you'll be making a huge mistake with those two."

"I can chose who I want in my bed."

"Whether it be one man or two?"

She dropped her gaze to the middle of his chest. "I'm sorry I've disappointed you."

With his fingers under her chin, he tipped her face up so he could see her eyes. "Aw, honey. You never could disappoint me. I'm afraid you'll get hurt in the long run with this whole thing, and I want nothing more than to protect you from it—but I can't, can I? You have to make your own mistakes in this life." He pulled her close and hugged her again. "I love you, Emma, and you'll always be my little girl, no matter how old you get. You do what makes you happy, honey. That's all I ask."

"Thanks, Dad. I love you, too." After a tight hug, she returned to the beer taps. Thankfully, Josh had disappeared into the crowd. God, she hated him with every fiber of her being.

Two years ago, they'd been one of the hottest items in Red Rock. Josh's daddy owned a good-sized spread outside of town, and he'd be set to inherit when his daddy passed on. Trouble was, Josh didn't care for ranching. All he wanted was the prestige of being a land owner, not the work involved in running cattle or anything else. Believing she could change his mind, she'd jumped into their relationship with both feet and huge blinders on. When he'd gotten down on one knee and asked her to marry him, the thrill of what she'd thought was love had driven her to say yes.

Then the rumors had started flying. His excuses had become disturbingly frequent. First he was working late, then he'd wanted to go out with the guys, or he'd had to make a trip into Billings for his dad. The last trip he'd made, she'd decided to surprise him—but *she* had gotten the bombshell when she'd walked into his hotel room to find him with Betty, buck-ass naked and tangled in the sheets. After she'd flung her engagement ring at him, she'd stormed out of the hotel and driven at breakneck speed to cry on her daddy's shoulder. Once she'd cried the hurt out, she'd proceeded to get stinking drunk. The next morning, the sun had crested over the mountains in a bright ray of light, wiping the misery and pain from her heart, leaving the headache of a hangover behind.

Since then, there hadn't been any serious relationship for her. Nope, the moment she'd heard Brandon's voice and gazed into those big brown eyes, she'd been hooked. Every show within a hundred miles found her there, in whatever seat she could get up close to the stage. Of course, Brandon had a gorgeous woman on his arm every moment, and Emma knew she could never compete with them. How she'd managed to snag both Beau and Brandon's attention, she wasn't sure, but she planned to ride it until they moved on.

"Emma?" Charlene's voice broke through her thoughts.

"Hi, honey. How are you feeling?" she asked, taking in the pale skin, dark circles under the little girl's eyes, and gaunt body. "You look fabulous. I bet Brandon could hardly talk, lookin' into those big green eyes of yours." Charlene held Brandon's guitar in her hands like she'd never let go.

Charlene giggled and shook her head. "He's so cute."

"I know, huh," Emma answered, wrapping her arm around Charlene's shoulders.

"He gave me his guitar."

"That is so cool. Are you gonna sell it? 'Cause if you are, I'm buying, honey."

Her eyes widened and she grasped the neck of the guitar harder. "No way! He signed it for me and everything." The little girl traced Brandon's signature and sighed. "I need to learn to play it, so someday when I see him again, I can play for him."

"I bet he'd love to hear you sing. You sing like an angel," Emma whispered, wiping the stray tear forming at the corner of her eye. If the rumors she heard were true, this poor little girl probably wouldn't even make it to her next birthday. The tumor in her brain continued to grow, killing more tissue every day, and they couldn't operate.

"I wanted to say thank you like my mom told me to."

"Thank you? For what, honey?"

"You made it possible for today to happen—for Brandon to be here to sing and all."

"Charlene, I think God had a hand in bringing Brandon and Beau here for you and for me."

The little girl hugged her waist, and Emma fought the tears she knew were just under the surface. "You love them, don't you?"

Shocked by Charlene's statement, Emma started to protest before realizing her little friend probably had more insight than she'd given Charlene credit for. "I'm not sure it's love, Charlene, but I sure like them a whole lot."

"Don't let the busybodies tell you who to love."

Emma couldn't help but smile at Charlene's words. The little girl had a valid point. "When did you get so grown up and so smart?"

Charlene shrugged and said, "I saw you dancin' with Brandon's brother when he sang. You looked happy."

"You're one special girl, Charlene, and I'm glad I know you."

"I love you, Emma, and I just know someday you'll wear the smile you had on earlier every day of your life." Charlene motioned for Emma to bend down and she kissed Emma on the cheek before rushing back to her parents' side.

The crowd in the beer tent thinned out after Brandon's concert, only a few patrons still lingered. Most wandered back out to the stands to watch the rest of the day's rodeo events. Beau and Brandon continued to break down the equipment and haul it outside while she watched.

Each man had his own style. Yes, they were identical, but the more she watched them, the more she realized how different they were. Beau's physique had a little more bulk across his back and shoulders, probably from riding bulls or working out, whereas Brandon seemed leaner. She knew they'd grown up in a small town in Montana, and their parents had cattle, too, like hers—but she didn't know exactly where. Beau seemed to be the epitome of a Montana cowboy. She had no doubt he would be a force to be reckoned with if he had rope to play with.

Rope? "Hmmm."

"What are you thinking, Emma? I see the sparkle in your eyes." Becky glanced to where Emma's gaze seemed glued. "Ah. That explains it. Those two seem to garner a lot of your attention."

"Look at them, Becky. The two of them are perfection—sexy in cowboy boots or out of them and so damned drool-worthy—who wouldn't want them?"

"Very true—even if they aren't my type, I have to agree with you." They both watched for a bit before Becky said, "You never did finish telling me about being with both of them."

"Not much else to tell. Having both men attuned to my needs? What else could a woman ask for?"

"So what happens now? I mean, they travel all the time. It's just a quick fling, right?"

Emma chewed the inside of her mouth for a second before she answered. "Yeah."

"You don't sound convinced, Emma Leanne."

"It doesn't matter. It's not like they went into this thing with me intending to make it a permanent threesome." A heavy sigh rushed from between her lips. "I can imagine the town gossips having a field day with that little tidbit."

"You know what? To hell with them, Emma. You need to do what's right for you. If being with those two gorgeous hunks of man flesh is what you want, then I say go for it."

"Really?" Emma asked, surprised Becky would support her being with two men. "I thought you would be totally not for this."

"Why?"

"Hello? Your daddy is a preacher, Becky. Hell, he didn't even want us to be friends since my parents weren't God-fearing churchgoers."

"I know, but *he's* the preacher, not me. I'm open to new things and trying to live my life the way I see fit, even if it means making him mad," Becky said, a small smile lighting her face and taking away the sadness Emma had seen there for so long.

Shock raced through her at Becky's words. "Are you going to date Seth?"

"Yes."

Emma squealed and hugged her friend tight. "I'm so happy for you! I think you two will make a great couple. Did this come about when he followed you outside?"

"Yeah. We finally talked heart to heart and I realized I was letting my father's beliefs ruin my chance to be with the man I wanted. Will it work into a long-term relationship? I don't know, but I'm willing to give it a try."

"Thank you, God!" Emma hugged Becky again. "I wondered when you would come to your senses."

* * * *

Beau watched Emma and her friend from his position near the stage. "The concert went great," Beau said, putting his hands behind his back and stretching. "Damn, I'm gonna be sore tomorrow. Ridin' the bull and hauling equipment—I haven't done this much manual labor in a while. I can tell I need to do some pushin' horns to get my strength back. At least I placed in the bull ridin' so I could donate it to Charlene."

"Yeah, I know the feeling. I got kinda used to havin' the road crew doin' all this. It's too bad they took a different route since we wanted to visit with Mom and Dad." Brandon glanced at the crates of equipment and sighed. "So how long are we plannin' on stayin' here, Beau?"

"As long as it takes."

"For what?"

"To convince Miss Emma she wants to be with us."

Brandon frowned. "I didn't think that was such a problem. She seemed into it enough when we were behind the stands."

Beau held his breath for a few seconds and then let it out slowly. His brother wasn't going to believe what he was about to say. "I don't mean be with us for the time we are here, Brandon, I mean permanently."

With Brandon's wide eyes and his mouth hanging open far enough he could catch flies, Beau had to work hard not to laugh. Brandon said, "No way. You, thinkin' seriously about a woman? Since when?"

"Since Emma."

"I don't know, Beau. A permanent triad?"

"We can work out the details another time. Right now, we need to convince her being with us is what she wants."

"I'm game. I'd love to have her with us all the time."

"Are you sure? I mean, Brandon Tucker with one woman?"

"If it's Emma, sure. Why not?" Brandon's nonchalant shrug didn't fool Beau. He knew his brother had feelings for Emma, too. Thoughts and feelings were one of those things being a twin came with. They could sense each other's thoughts and feelings, and Beau knew exactly Brandon's feelings on the matter of Emma Weston.

"Then we need a plan. I want tonight with her alone."

"Why you? Why not me?"

"Remember our bet? She screamed my name first."

"Oh all right, fine." The scowl on Brandon's face almost made Beau laugh. He knew his brother didn't like being pushed aside, even by him. "But I get her tomorrow then."

"What are you two plannin' over here?" Emma asked, walking up behind them.

"Us? Nothin', darlin'," Beau said, sliding an arm around her waist. "You did agree to some more time with us tonight, remember?"

Her fingers did a little dance down the front of his chest, playing with the buttons on his shirt. "Yes I did, and since most of the festivities are over with for tonight, except for some rowdy party crowd drinkin' too much beer, I'm ready to go."

"I tell you what, sweetheart, I'm going to stay here and mingle some more while you and Beau have some time alone."

"Seriously?" she asked, her eyes widening into almost saucers. "Why?"

"I asked Brandon to let me have some one-on-one time with you," Beau replied. "He'll join us after while. How about we have a nice dinner somewhere, and then we can do whatever you want."

"Whatever I want?"

"Yep."

"This could be exciting." She stepped out of his embrace and leaned over to kiss Brandon on the cheek. "We'll try not to have too much fun without you." When she turned back toward Beau, she asked, "Just out of curiosity, do you happen to have some rope?"

Rope? "Now, what would I be needin' rope for, darlin'?"

"Oh, I don't know. Maybe I want you to tie me up and have your way with me," she said, wrapping her arms around his neck and pressing her lips to the base of his throat where his heart pounded.

Brandon hissed through his teeth at Emma's words. Beau knew his brother had a kinky side, and he'd never found anyone he could connect with on that level. For both their sakes, he prayed Emma would be the one.

"I think I can find some," he growled. Need spiked hard at her saucy words. He'd like nothing better than to tie her spread-eagle on the bed and do anything he wanted to with her delectable body.

"Let's get this party started then." With her hand in his, they left Brandon in the beer tent and walked to where a truck was parked. "How about we take mine, but you can drive?"

"You got it fixed already?"

"Not exactly. It's my dad's. He doesn't like me out drivin' late at night in the car. The truck is bigger. "

"Great! Where's a good place for dinner?"

"Depends on how much money you want to spend wining and dining me, handsome."

"Your choice, darlin'. Whatever you want."

"Hmm." She tapped her fingers to her lips as thoughts zipped across her eyes in a pattern he could almost interpret. "How about we drive a little ways? There's a town about twenty minutes from here with a really nice restaurant."

"Sounds good to me."

"I want to run by my Dad's place and take a quick shower. I smell like beer and cigarettes."

"Sure, darlin'," he replied, although he wasn't sure he wanted to be cornered by her pa and her brother. "How about after you shower and change, we head back to the hotel so I can do the same? I smell like cattle. I hope this place isn't too fancy. I don't think I brought anything with me to fit in somewhere like that."

Ten minutes later he sat in her daddy's living room while she showered and changed upstairs.

"You're takin' Emma out for dinner?" her father asked, tapping his fingers on the arm of the leather chair.

"Yes, sir. She mentioned a place in a town about twenty minutes away."

"Probably Red's in Watertown. It's the best steak house around."

"Yes, sir." Damn, he sounded like a teenager being grilled by his date's father.

The older man's eyes narrowed and the tapping on the arm of the chair increased in tempo.

"If there is somethin' you want to say, sir, please do."

"All right then, I will. My daughter means the world to me, Mr. Tucker, and I hope you treat her with respect. She can be impetuous."

"Yeah, she mentioned it."

"What I'm trying to say is, I know about her having sex with both you and your brother."

Beau felt like something sat on his chest. *Aw, hell.*

"And I don't approve of her relationship with you. But, it appears you and Brandon will only be in town a short time, so I will tolerate your presence until you leave. Do I make myself clear?"

"Yes, sir."

"Good."

"Can I say one thing, Mr. Weston?"

"Certainly."

"I care about Emma and wouldn't do anything to hurt her."

"But you will, Mr. Tucker. I've seen your type before. You roll into town like a tumbleweed with no place to anchor itself. You flash your money and your smile, expecting the women to fall at your feet—and they do. Women in these small towns don't have a ton of men to choose from when they seek out a partner for life. But you are not *husband* material."

"I respect your opinion, but you don't know me at all. I travel with my brother because he's my brother, and I promised him I would be by his side while he builds his career. I don't plan to live the way I do for the rest of my life."

"What are your plans then?"

"I bought a piece of property, and within the next couple of years I want to raise buckin' bulls for the rodeo on it. My parents raised us on a ranch, and pushin' horns is what I know."

"I heard your rode bulls." Mitchell Weston's eyebrows drew together and he frowned.

"Sometimes. It's more of a hobby than a career for me."

"Good to know." The frown on her father's face loosened a bit, and Beau breathed a little easier. "Rodeoin' isn't quite the glamorous life it's made out to be, especially if there's a woman involved right along with the rider."

"No, it's not, Mr. Weston."

"Dad, quit grillin' Beau. It's only a dinner date," Emma said as she walked into the living room.

The black strapless dress hugged her curves in all the right places and made his mouth water. It brushed her legs at mid-thigh, tempting him almost beyond his control to taste, touch, and explore.

A raging hard-on in front of her dad is not the way to impress the man.

"Maybe," her father replied, rubbing the stubble on his chin. "I just like to know somethin' about the men my daughter dates. Is it a crime to care these days?"

She leaned down and kissed him on the cheek. "No, Dad, it's not." A quick wink in Beau's direction revealed her impish nature. "I'll be home late, so don't wait up."

"You're coming home?" he asked, clearly not believing she didn't plan to stay out all night.

"I don't know for sure, but I don't want you waiting and then me not showing up at all."

"All right, Emma, but be careful, huh?" he said, hugging her, but staring Beau down over the top of her head.

"I will, Dad. I love you."

"I love you, too, Emma."

Beau scrambled to his feet, relieved the interrogation was over for now. Somehow he knew he wasn't out of the woods yet with her father. Mr. Weston seemed the type to expect a ring on his little girl's finger before things got hot and heavy again. *How would he feel about Emma being with both me and Brandon as a permanent triad?*

Protectiveness, mistrust, and suspicion swirled in her father's gaze when it met Beau's again, and Beau swallowed hard.

Chapter Ten

The lights of Watertown twinkled in the distance as Beau drove Emma's truck down the highway. Tires hummed against the blacktop, lulling her and relaxing her tense shoulders. Catching her Dad grilling Beau made her worry. The last thing she wanted was her father messing up this little rendezvous with Beau and Brandon. If she only had a few days to store away memories, she'd take what she could get.

She'd picked this restaurant for two reasons. One, the food would make anyone's mouth water, and two, there wouldn't be too many folks from Red Rock around—she hoped.

"What are you thinkin' about, darlin'?" Beau asked, grasping her fingers and then entwining them with his own.

"I hope my dad's question and answer session didn't piss you off."

"Nah. He's worried about you. I can't blame him." He glanced her way and then back out the windshield. "How did he find out about our threesome?"

"My big mouth."

"Huh?"

"My ex-fiancé cornered me at the beer taps, and he said some things about you and Brandon. I informed him whether we'd slept together or not was none of his business. My dad overheard the conversation and asked me point blank if we'd slept together. I couldn't lie, so I told him yes." The concerned look on Beau's face sent apprehension down her spine. "It's okay though. He understood."

"To a point, I think he does, but he definitely thinks the less time you spend with us, the better for you."

"He just wants to protect me."

"I know," he murmured, bringing her fingers to his lips and nibbling on the tips. "It's what fathers do."

"Brothers too."

"True. Cade is protective of you."

Several moments of silence passed while she thought about Brandon's story in relation to her own siblings. A sister. She smiled at the thought of them protecting a cute little girl with features similar to theirs. Having brothers herself, she knew how they could be with their siblings—teasing them one moment and ready to punch anyone who hurt them, the next. "I'm sorry about your sister."

"Thanks. It happened a long time ago, but Bailey's always in our thoughts."

"She had cancer?"

"Yeah. Acute Lymphoblastic Leukemia. She'd been sick since she turned a year old and we always knew she probably wouldn't make it to adulthood. The outcome for her type of cancer didn't bode well."

"Was she older than you?"

A heavy sigh escaped his lips, bringing her attention to their fullness and her need to taste him. "We were actually triplets. She was the third born, a few minutes after Brandon."

"Wow."

"Bailey had chromosomal problems from the beginning. She had Down's Syndrome, too, but she was our third." He inhaled a deep cleansing breath and continued. "Our mother had a real hard time with it—always blaming herself."

"She couldn't control those things."

"I know, and so do you, but when it's something like that…"

The need to take away some of his pain enveloped her heart. Even though she fought with her siblings, she couldn't imagine her life without one of them in it. Cade took care of all of them, and Sharon, the oldest girl, took over the motherly duties when their mom died a few years ago, but she had her own family. Elizabeth was the nosy one—always in everyone's business, but she meant well. Being the youngest sister, Emma got the brunt of their protectiveness, but then they had Jarrod. He got all of it, being the baby of the family. Spoiled, mothered by the sisters, and so handsome women came easy to him, he could have any woman he wanted. Emma knew someday he'd run into a girl who would throw him for a loop, and he wouldn't know what hit him.

All the thoughts of siblings and family made Emma feel closer to Beau than she had before. She laid her head on his shoulder and silently tried to absorb all his hurt and pain. He'd suffered so much loss. Losing a sibling probably hurt as much, if not more, than losing a parent. "I can't even imagine the pain you went through, Beau."

"You lost your mom not long ago, didn't you?" he asked, unlacing their fingers and wrapping his arm around her shoulders to pull her closer.

Emma sniffed and tried to hold back the tears burning her throat and choking her words. She missed her mom every day, but today seemed worse. The mention of Beau and Brandon's sister brought home the pain and loss she felt. "Yeah. She was hit by a drunk driver and killed."

"I'm sorry."

"It's okay," she whispered and then cleared her throat. After a moment, she went on. "It still hurts. She'll never see me marry. She'll never see her grandchildren or great-grandchildren, and I know she looked forward to bouncing them on her knee. Cade's little boy, Alan, hadn't been born yet. Only one of my sisters is already married. Elizabeth and I aren't, and right now, there isn't any prospect of a husband anywhere within several hundred miles. Red Rock isn't a beehive of eligible bachelors, if you hadn't noticed."

"True, but I'm sure there's someone you might think would make good husband material, right?"

"Yeah, but the last thing on their minds…uh…his mind…is marriage, or even a steady girlfriend, I'm sure." The lights of Watertown came into sharp view as they reached the city limits. "Turn right at the stop sign. The restaurant is on the next block." Emma, growing uncomfortable with the conversation, was glad of a change of subject. Thinking long-term with Beau and Brandon wasn't the wisest thing to do.

Beau parked the truck, hopped out, and then came around to open her door. *Such a gentleman.*

She stepped out of the truck, and he wrapped an arm around her shoulders as he pushed the door shut.

"Have I told you how nice you look?"

"No, you haven't, Mr. Tucker," she quipped, glancing up at him through her lashes.

"I could eat you up. You look fabulous in that pretty, figuring-hugging black dress," he murmured by her ear and then nipped at the lobe. "I can't wait to get you alone."

"Promise?"

"I'll promise anything if you keep lookin' at me with those sexy eyes."

"Be careful. You never know the things I might force you to promise if you give me the chance."

"Bring it on, babe."

The warm chuckle he punctuated his words with had desire sizzling across her skin. *Was it only this morning we made love?* Made love? No, had sex. She must think of it as having sex.

"What's the pretty blush for?" he asked, guiding her toward the hostess.

"Mmm. Wouldn't you like to know?"

The restaurant boasted a western motif, including old lanterns, antique washboards, signs, wagon wheels, and western tack hung from the walls and ceiling. Country music played softly from the overhead speakers and she absently wondered if they'd hear one of Brandon's songs while they were there.

Beau's lips brushed her neck, and he whispered, "I *will* extract payment for that little smartass comment, Miss Emma."

A thrill of fear followed by the zing of desire had her pussy throbbing to the increased rate of her heart. "I can't wait." *Holy hell! Did I just say that? And what if Beau actually ties me to the bed? Or better, pulls me over his knee and spanks me?*

He cleared his throat as they reached their booth, and he let her slide in before sitting down himself. Together, they only took up a small portion of the horseshoe-shaped bench. A quick glance at his cock before he took his seat revealed his erection pressing against the front of his jeans, and she had to hide her smile.

The waitress introduced herself and gave Beau several bold looks. Emma seethed with frustration and jealousy, although Beau acted the perfect gentleman, never once giving the waitress any encouragement. *I can't believe we ran into her. I can't catch a break here. The one woman who hates me more than anything on this earth, and she has to be our waitress. I hope she doesn't poison my food or something, but I wouldn't put it past her to dump it into my lap—and all over a guy in high school.*

Emma busied herself looking at the menu and pouted while she listened to Beau order a bottle of wine and an appetizer.

"Are you hungry?" he asked, sliding his fingers along the top of her hand.

"Yes, actually. I'm starvin'. I didn't get to eat much after breakfast at the diner, and there usually isn't time while we're servin' folks during the rodeo," she replied, folding the menu and placing it on the table.

"So what are you going to order? At your dad's the other night, you were a hearty eater."

"You noticed how I ate?"

"Sure. I like women who eat normal and don't pick at their food."

She laughed and picked up a peanut from the bucket on the table. Cracking it open with a loud pop, she stuffed the insides into her mouth and tossed the shell on the floor. "I don't think anyone ever said I picked at my food. I eat whatever is put in front of me usually. There isn't much I don't like."

He leaned in from his position next to her and whispered against her ear, "We didn't get to use the strawberries and whipped cream the kitchen sent up. I'd love to lick them off your breasts."

Her nipples drew into hard nubs, tingling and throbbing at his words.

"You like the sound of that, huh? Your nipples are hard just thinking about it."

His hard body blocked anyone from seeing what he did as his fingers plucked at the tip pressing against her dress. The ache of need grew to desperate proportions. The need to have his mouth on her exploded into heart-pounding, pussy creaming desire, and if he didn't knock it off, she'd ride his hips right here.

"Have you ever been tied spread-eagle on a bed?"

"No," she squeaked, imaging herself stretched out and open to his every whim. The mere thought ramped up her desire as she shifted on the seat.

"Open for me. Unable to stop me from doing anything to you I want to. Bringing you to orgasm multiple times with my mouth and tongue." The low growl of his sexy voice, punctuated by several small licks on her skin, and she was ready to do anything he wanted—anything.

Shit! He's killin' me here.

"Licking every inch of your incredible skin. Sucking on your nipples until they're pebble-hard. My cock is so hard for you, it's killin' me." The warm wetness of his tongue played with her earlobe. "Are you hot and wet, Emma?"

The answer eluded her. Her brain turned to mush the moment he'd mentioned *spread-eagle on a bed*. She couldn't think—could barely breathe beyond short gasps.

His hand snaked beneath the tablecloth and shimmied up her skirt to find her naked thigh. The urge to spread her legs and give him unbridled access rushed through her body, taking away any thoughts of denying him.

"Oh God." Her words came out in small pants as she struggled to pull enough air into her lungs to keep from passing out.

"Such a naughty girl, you are. No panties."

One finger brushed her clit, and she almost sank beneath the table.

"Do you want me to touch you, Emma?" he asked in a low purr that reverberated along her nerve-endings.

She whimpered and closed her eyes.

"I'll take that as a yes." Two fingers slid into her pussy. "You're so wet. God, you're driving me crazy."

Her head fell back against his shoulder, and she spread her thighs farther apart.

"Do you want me to make you come?"

"Here?" she whispered, while her pussy sucked at his fingers. A quick glance at the tables nearby revealed their seclusion and the sides of the booth were high enough, no one could see what naughtiness was transpiring within their little world.

"Do you think you can be quiet?"

"I don't…"

His thumb circled her clit, and his fingers continued to push in and out of her pussy. "Come for me, darlin'."

He covered her mouth as she came apart in his arms, stifling her cry of climax with his lips. Public exhibitionism wasn't her thing, but right now, she couldn't care less who knew she'd just climaxed because this gorgeous man had finger fucked her until she couldn't hold back.

Beau finally lifted his head, staring down at her with those fathomless brown eyes. "Better?"

With her breath still coming in sharp pants, she couldn't answer except to nod her head, eliciting a wicked smile from the man responsible.

"There's more where that came from."

"Can we leave now?"

"Impatient?"

"Hell yeah. Appetizers are great, but I'm lookin' for the whole meal."

His roar of laughter brought stares and frowns from some of the other patrons of the restaurant, but Emma frowned right back at them and then kissed Beau on the lips.

"I hope I don't have a wet spot on the back of my dress," she said, sneaking one of the napkins beneath the table to wipe the cream from her thighs and pussy.

"I'll walk behind you, just in case."

A quick glance revealed his wicked smirk had returned. "Right. You want to walk behind me to check out my ass."

"Somethin' wrong with lookin' at your fine ass?"

The waitress returned with their appetizer and all but threw the plate on the table with a loud bang. She shot Emma a scathing look, turned on her heel, and stomped away.

"I think she's a little pissed," Emma said, snagging a deep fried mushroom and dipping it into the ranch dressing. "God, I love these." She licked her fingers very slowly, teasing Beau. Two could fool around at this foreplay thing.

One dark masculine eyebrow shot up, and his eyes darkened to almost black.

"Horny, honey?"

"My dick is so hard, it would shatter if you put too much pressure on my zipper."

"Oh…let's see." She pressed her palm to his cock and sighed.

"Emma," he growled, grabbing her hand and pressing it harder against his dick.

"You made me come. I should give you the same consideration, Beau," she murmured, unbuttoning and unzipping his jeans. His cock sprang free, and he groaned low in his throat. "My, my. All this for me?"

"You know it is. I want to be buried in your sweet heat right now, not coming in your hand."

"How about if I play a little?" she asked, running her fingernail down the length of his cock and back up.

"You're gonna pay for this later, Emma. I'm gonna torture you until you beg," he growled. The quick flick of his tongue over his lips gave away the tight rein of control he must be hoping to hold onto while she tortured him.

"Another promise? I'm likin' this." Wrapping her fingers around his cock, she did a slow slide up and down. "So smooth and hard at the same time." Her thumb spread the pre-cum from the tip of his penis around and around the head as she watched his face flush. She wanted to lick the thick salty liquid, but unless she ducked under the table, it would be impossible. The thought intrigued her.

The small lift of his hips toward her hand told her he barely hung onto his self-control, and she wanted to take it away from him so badly, she could taste it—and taste it she would.

* * * *

The little witch was going to kill him. Her warm palm caressed his cock slowly, rubbing, encircling, and grasping it until he thought he might die. He knew he probably deserved her torture after forcing her to climax in the middle of the restaurant, and he could tell she planned to pay him back in spades.

A wicked grin spread across her lips, and he knew he didn't stand a chance. One beautifully arched eyebrow cocked saucily at him before she disappeared beneath the table.

Aw, fuck!

Her warm mouth closed over the head of his cock, and he almost shot his load right there. Oh, she would pay for this later—no doubt about it—but right now, he savored her tongue swirling around his cock and the tight confines of her mouth when she sucked.

"Sir, can I get you anything else at the moment? Your dinner should be ready soon," the waitress said, glancing at the now empty booth.

"N-no." The high pitch squeak of his voice made him cringe. He cleared his throat to try again. "No. We're doin' fine, thanks." Emma sucked the head of his cock into her mouth and deep throated him. He fought the need to close his eyes while the waitress stood there staring at him. "Water. Yeah, water would be great."

"Of course," she replied and cocked her head to the side like she wanted to say something more before she walked away.

He fought for breath while Emma continued to torment him. His balls were on fire. His dick ached with the need to come. The soft slide of her tongue had his legs trembling. As his climax drew closer, he grabbed a napkin off the table and shoved it beneath the tablecloth, unsure whether she planned to swallow or not.

The little napkin popped back up his stomach and waved like a white flag. Beau looked around to see if anyone watched the goings-on in their booth, and thankfully, everyone seemed occupied with their own conversations.

Unable to fight her loving care anymore, he gripped the tabletop and bit the inside of his cheek as cum shot out of the end of his dick, Emma's eager mouth swallowing every drop.

Several moments later, Emma returned to her seat with a cheeky grin on her lips while he tried to discreetly zip up his pants.

"Emma Leanne Weston. How the hell are you, honey?"

A stout older woman, probably in her eighties, stopped at their table. Her pure white hair, styled into a fashionable bun at the back of her head, gave away her age, but the mischievous twinkle in her blue eyes and the smile on her lips said she lived life to the fullest. "Gram!" Emma slid out of the booth and hugged the old woman tight enough, Beau heard her bones creak. Beau sighed in relief when he managed to get his zipper up without giving too much away—he hoped.

"Easy, Emma, honey. These old bones can't handle all the huggin'." She glanced at him and grinned. "Who's the hunk?"

Emma laughed and sat back down. "Gram, this is Beau Tucker. Beau this is Gram. No, she's not my real grandmother, but she adopted the Weston bunch when Natalie married Cade. She's actually Natalie's grandmother."

"Nice to meet you, ma'am." He jumped to his feet, indicating she could sit. "Would you like to join us?"

"I'd love to, you sexy man, you, but I have a date." The cheeky grin on the old woman's face was priceless.

"A date?" Emma asked, her eyes the size of saucers.

"Yes. I'm meeting Samuel Johnson for dinner."

"Isn't he your attorney?"

"Yes he is, you nosy girl," Gram replied, although the twinkle in her eyes belied her words.

Emma laughed.

"No matchmakin', do you hear me, Emma?"

"I didn't say anythin'."

"I know you didn't, but I can see the sparkle in your eyes—or did your handsome escort put it there?"

Beau couldn't believe his ears. It appeared the old woman had a huge sense of humor, and she obviously had no qualms about saying what came to mind.

"I'd have to say Beau put it there, Gram."

"I'll tell you the same thing I told Natalie when she started datin' Cade. I hope you have condoms in your purse, because it doesn't appear to me your young man will be keepin' his hands to himself for very long."

Beau choked on his water. If she only knew where both of their hands had been in the last half an hour, she'd probably have a stroke right then.

Gram smacked him on the back several times between the shoulder blades.

"You gonna live, young man? 'Cause if you aren't, you best pay the tab right now."

Emma rolled her eyes and giggled.

"I'm okay. Thanks," he choked out and then coughed again.

"Good. You look like a strappin' lad. What do you do for a livin'?" Gram asked, apparently deciding to join them for a few moments after all as she scooted in next to Emma.

"I currently work as a road manager for my brother."

"Your brother?" Gram asked.

"Yes, ma'am. My brother is Brandon Tucker, the country music artist."

"I thought you looked familiar. Isn't he the face you have on your wall, Emma?"

Emma rolled her eyes and sighed. "Yes, Gram, he is. Beau and Brandon are identical twins."

"Well, holy hell on a stick! There are two of them? Hot damn! Two gorgeous hunks like that one there ought to keep you busy for awhile."

Beau laughed and shook his head. He loved Emma's Gram already.

"Gram, please." Emma tried to shush her, looking around. The other diners had begun looking at them curiously.

"Ah, don't worry about them, Emma honey. They're all jealous of the good lookin' couple you make. I'd sure like to see you sandwiched between him and his twin. Wouldn't that be one hell of a sight?"

An elderly gentleman walked up to their table and addressed Gram. "Mrs. Oliver, why don't we take our business to this other table over here?"

"Oh, go on with you, Sam. If you want to go sit, then go sit your ass down. You're an old fuddy-duddy anyway. This here is my granddaughter and her date. I'm talkin' to them for a minute."

"I see. Well, join me then when you're through," he replied, moving off to sit at a table several feet away with an annoyed look on his face.

"Now, where were we?" She tapped her gnarled finger on the table. "Oh yeah, you between him and his brother. I think you'd make a cute threesome. Did I ever tell you how Natalie's mother dated your dad and the idiot she married?"

The waitress arrived with their dinner plates, and Beau hoped Gram might take her leave, but she started talking about her daughter dating two men during high school, and then how Cade, Natalie, and Kale had dated when Natalie arrived in town. It sounded to Beau like the whole place liked threesomes. One could always hope.

"Are you plannin' on settlin' down in Red Rock, son?" Gram asked.

"I'm not sure what my plans are past next month, to tell you the truth. It's important for me to be there for my brother."

Gram nodded and pursed her lips. "I understand the family thing. I sure do—but what about Emma?"

"Gram, I think I can take care—"

"Nonsense. Let me do the negotiatin' here," she said interrupting Emma's words. "Just how do you feel about my granddaughter?"

"Gram, we've only known each other a few days."

"And that means what? Grandpa Oliver told me he loved me the night of our second date. He asked me to marry him one week after we started going steady, and we were married sixty-eight years when he passed on." Gram narrowed her eyes and stared him down. He felt like an insect on a microscope slide while she chewed on whatever she would say next. After several minutes, she nodded and rose to her feet.

"You love her. I can see it in your eyes. You best be makin' an honest woman of my Emma, or you won't want to be anywhere near Red Rock, Montana for the next hundred years or so. See, I plan to haunt people who hurt my family, and Emma is family." Two quick taps of her cane on the floor and she said, "I best get a weddin' invitation." She turned to Emma next. "I want to meet his brother, too. Plan on Sunday dinner at my house, and bring 'em both."

Beau sat with his mouth open watching the feisty old woman walk away. "What the hell just happened?"

"My Gram happened. You have to kind of ignore her. She tends to be very bold and outspoken."

"I really couldn't tell," he replied, chuckling. "She's great."

"I'm glad you think so. Most guys I've dated couldn't handle her."

"I don't know why. She's a breath of fresh air."

Emma frowned and played with her fork, twirling it between her fingers. She apparently had something on her mind and he wondered what as he watched uncertainty and worry, zip across her eyes.

"What's wrong?" Beau asked.

"I love her to death, but I'm sorry she put you on the spot."

He took her hand in his and kissed her fingertips. "Its fine, Emma. I would love havin' her around all the time. She would definitely keep us on our toes."

"She definitely keeps us wonderin'."

A frown settled on his mouth. "What else is bothering you?"

Her bottom lip disappeared between her teeth, and Beau knew she had something on her mind. "Is what she said true?"

"What did she say?"

"She said you love me." Hope and fear laced her words, and he wondered if Emma wanted him to love her or not.

Chapter Eleven

His Adam's apple bobbed up and down nervously. "Well, I, uh…"

The inability to answer her question told her he either didn't love her or hadn't even thought about it. Either way, she needed to let him off the hook and bury her disappointment. "Never mind, Beau. It was a stupid thing to ask. I mean, we've only known each other a few days, and people don't fall in love in two days."

Beau took her hands in his and squeezed them. "You are an amazing woman, Emma, and I love spendin' time with you, makin' love to you, and watchin' you take life by the horns, but *in love*? I don't know how to answer you."

"You just did, and it's fine, really."

The caress of his hand against hers almost brought her to tears. She wanted him to love her. She wanted both of them to love her, but she knew their lives held different goals. The road called to the two of them, whereas she needed stability...a home...a family.

"I care about you," he went on. "You've come to mean a lot to me in the few short days we've known each other, and I don't want to hurt you. My life is on the road with Brandon, at least for now."

"I know," she whispered, slowly tugging her hands from his. "When the bus is fixed and you two go on your merry way, I'll miss you." Almost losing her nerve, she caught his gaze with hers and then lowered it to where her clasped hands lay on the tabletop. "Both of you. And every time I see Brandon's face on my wall at home, I'll think of you and him. People may think you two are alike, but I've seen the differences—and I don't mean only intimately, although there's differences there, too."

Grasping her hands again, he brought them to his lips and kissed her knuckles. "Listen, Emma. I don't want to waste our time left together on talk of somethin' only God knows the outcome of. Let's make the most of it. Let me love you."

She inhaled a slow, easy breath and nodded. At least she could show him how much she cared with her body. It didn't matter whether she knew the outcome of their time together. The need for Beau and Brandon simply had to be fulfilled.

The snooty waitress arrived with the bill, and Beau laid out a debit card.

"Are you Brandon Tucker's brother? You look so much like him, it's scary."

"Yes, I am."

"Wow. I mean you two could be twins."

"We are."

"Seriously? I didn't know he had a twin, and I'm like his biggest fan ever. Can you introduce me to him? I'd be forever in your debt," the waitress gushed. "I'd make it worth your while." Her fingers trailed up Beau's arm, and Emma wanted to tear her limb from limb.

"I'm sorry but no. I'm out with my…"

"She doesn't matter."

"Excuse me?" Beau said with a low snarl. "Emma does matter. She's the only one who matters at the moment. Now please, get our tab taken care of so we can leave. And you can be sure I'll report your behavior to the management."

Shock and indignation swept across her face as she planted her hands on her hips. "Well, I never."

"I'm sure you have, actually." He turned to Emma, reached for her hand.

The waitress huffed and narrowed her eyes. Without another word, she headed back toward the kitchen, her shoulders back and her hips swinging as if to entice Beau away from Emma.

"God, I hate her," Emma said.

"Why? She's jealous of you."

"Little town, Beau. She's been a bitch ever since high school. Hatred's run deep between us ever since one of her boyfriends dumped her to go out with me."

The waitress returned with his receipt. "Here you go, handsome," she said, bending over far enough her tits practically spilled out of her top. "Sign right there, honey, and you'll be all set."

Beau grabbed the paper, wrote a big fat zero under the tip, signed his name and handed it back. "Come on, Emma. Let's get out of here before I do somethin' I'm gonna regret."

As they headed for the door, Emma heard behind her, "Can you believe that jerk? He didn't even leave me a tip, and I kissed his ass—or I would have, literally, if Emma the slut wasn't with him."

Emma stiffened, and Beau stopped to whisper in her ear. "Easy, darlin'. I'm leavin' with you, remember?"

"I'll be right back, Beau." He grabbed her hand to stop her from leaving, but she needed to do this. "It's fine." After a quick kiss to his lips, she pulled away and walked back toward the waitress. "Stacey, can I talk to you a moment?"

The other woman's eyebrow rose, and she flipped her hair over her shoulder. "What do you want?"

"I need to set the record straight. The only reason you're pissed off at me is because Greg left you for me back in high school. Don't you think it's time to get over this petty jealousy?" Emma asked sweetly. Kill 'em with kindness, her momma always said, although she wouldn't mind raking her nails down the bitch's face.

"Whatever, Emma. I could care less about Greg the loser," Stacey said with a bored, I-don't-give-a-shit look.

Emma lifted her chin and stared right into Stacey's eyes. "All right. I'm gonna share a little secret with you. Brandon wouldn't be interested in you anyway."

"Why not?" Stacey asked, placing her hands on her hips.

"Because he has me."

"What? You're datin' both of them?" Stacey looked like she could spit nails.

Emma nodded and smiled. "And you know what else? I've had sex with both of them…together."

"See, I knew you were a slut! Screwing both of them? God, what a whore!"

"Might be, Stacey, but I'm theirs. You aren't, and you'll never be." She spun around, presenting the still-sputtering Stacey with her back as she walked back to Beau. "I'm ready."

"What did you say to her?" he asked, placing his hand at the small of her back and escorting her out of the door.

"I belong to you and Brandon, and she never will."

"You don't care whether people know you're datin' both of us?"

After the visit with her Gram, Emma's feelings and thoughts on the matter had changed. Beau and Brandon were gorgeous, single and attracted to her. She wanted them, and she didn't care who knew it. Gossipmongers would have a field day, but eventually something else would happen, and the talk about her, Beau, and Brandon would disappear. "Nope, not anymore. I'm not going to hide and pretend it didn't happen. I'm proud you and Brandon want me. If the biddies and gossips in Red Rock don't like it, too bad."

A smile spread across his lips, and he bent down to brush them over hers. "I'm glad I'm on your side, Emma." They walked to where her truck sat parked in the lot. "Why don't you drive back?"

His request brought her to a stop, and she glanced at him, wondering whether he might be up to somethin'. The plan she'd had for the drive back would be ruined if she drove. "Are you sure? It's fine if you want to drive."

"No, you go ahead."

With a shrug, she walked around to the driver's side and slipped inside the cab. The truck started with a grumble as Beau buckled his belt and relaxed against the seat. "Where are we headed?"

"I'm sure there's a back way to get to Red Rock."

"There is, but why?"

A sexy-as-sin grin spread across his mouth, and she began to wonder if he didn't have a plan of his own. Damn, the man could make her hot with a simple look. After she squirmed and squeezed her pussy muscles together to try to relieve some of the pressure building in her groin, she reversed out of the parking lot.

When the lights of Watertown had faded in the rearview mirror, Beau unhooked his seat belt and slid to the center of the truck. The warmth of his palm caressed her bare thigh as he pushed up the hem of her dress, sending goose bumps from her toes to her scalp. The lump clogging her throat threatened to strangle her as her palms gripped the steering wheel.

Beau dropped his cowboy hat on the seat next to him and leaned toward her. "Are you hot, Emma?"

She couldn't say a word, only whimper.

His fingers stroked higher up her thigh, and she spread her legs to give him access to her pussy if he wanted to go all the way. God, she hoped he went all the way.

"Do you want me to touch you?" he whispered into her ear.

His breath ruffled the fine hairs near her temple, and shivers raced down her spine.

"Pleeeaase…"

"Oh, I love when you beg, babe."

His fingertips brushed the curls guarding her pussy. Seconds later, one found her clit and brushed it lightly.

"Find somewhere to pull off, Emma."

"I can't. It's ranch property," she whispered, desperately looking for a turn off. "Wait! There." An aluminum livestock gate blocked the entrance to the field.

"I'll open the gate. Pull behind the stand of trees to the left there."

"Someone might see us if they drive by."

"The truck will hide us from prying eyes. I want you, Emma, right now—and darlin', I plan on takin' you." As she stopped the truck, Beau slid out of the cab and slammed the door. The echo of the sound bounced around the cab, but the hard thump of her heart almost drowned out any other noise. Once the gate was open, she pulled through, and Beau closed it behind them.

She stopped the truck next to the trees and cut the engine. Beau stood outside by the passenger side and motioned with his finger for her to come around to his side. The twinkle in his brown eyes and the I-gonna-fuck-you smile on his lips had her pussy creaming before she ever got out of the truck. A quick shaky inhalation and then a long sigh helped a little, but the moment he touched her, the calm would disappear like a cloud of smoke.

When she rounded the back of the truck and the passenger side came into view, Beau stood with his arm propped on the now-open door and one booted foot crossed over the other. He held out his hand, and when she placed her palm in his, he slowly drew her closer.

"This is gonna be fun."

"What do you plan to do?" she asked, nervously glancing over her shoulder at the road and then back to him. Even if no one could see them, anyone passing from Red Rock would know this truck.

"You'll see."

The anticipation would kill her if he drew this out too long. She could already feel cream dripping down the inside of her thigh.

"Sit on the seat with your butt on the edge and spread those gorgeous thighs for me."

The warmth of the evening air on her wet, bare pussy made her breath catch in her throat. Cool leather felt strange against her butt when she sat down and spread her legs. He knelt on the running board and leaned forward. The seat height lined him up perfectly to eat her pussy until she came all over his face. The moment Beau's tongue touched her clit, she bit back a scream of ecstasy.

"So wet," he murmured, kissing the inside of her thigh as he shoved a finger deep into her vagina. "All for me."

The wet slide of his tongue from vagina to clit felt like heaven—Beau's kind of heavenly torture. "You're killin' me, Beau."

"Relax, darlin'."

His tongue did several figure eights on her clit before he sucked it between his lips and shoved two fingers into her pussy.

Her breathing came in small pants as she tried desperately to forestall the rising climax he pulled from deep inside her, but it was no use. He had her in the palm of his hand, ready to beg for what she wanted.

"God, Beau, please. I need to come so bad."

The speed of his fingers and tongue stoked her climax and held her on the edge by her fingernails. She whimpered and begged, but every time she got there, he'd slow his strokes until she calmed, and then he'd bring her right back up.

Unable to stand his fantastic torture any longer, she grabbed both of his ears in her fingers and pinched.

"Ouch!"

"If…you…don't…make…me…come…I'm going to torture you by staking your ass out in the hot sun and leaving you to the fire ants."

"A little on edge, darlin'?"

"A lot on edge, Beau. Stop teasing me. I can't stand it anymore."

He stood up and reached into his back pocket for his wallet. With a wicked grin, he tore open the condom he'd retrieved and rolled it over his erection.

"Hurry." Both hands grasped her hips as she reclined on the seat. One hard thrust and he was buried balls-deep inside her pussy. "Ah!"

After Beau released a sharp hiss, his hips started the steady rhythm she knew would throw her over in half a second. When he drew his thumb over her clit and then pressed down hard, she flew apart with a shattering scream that echoed in the silence around them.

"One," he whispered, the hard thrust of his hips never stopping, until she hung on the edge a second time. "Come for me again, darlin'. Squeeze my cock like a vice, Emma. I need to feel you milkin' me for everythin' I've got."

His sexy talk and pounding rhythm threw her into a second climax big enough to rival anything she'd had before. Stars danced behind her eyelids, her chest hurt from breathing so fast, and her whole body tingled as Beau groaned her name and came right along with her.

* * * *

They returned to Beau and Brandon's suite after their torrid romp in the middle of God only knew whose pasture, only to find Brandon still out. Burying the feelings of jealousy deep inside, she dragged Beau into the bathroom, turned on the huge bathtub, and ripped his shirt off with one quick tug.

After they made love in the bathtub, Beau swept her up in his arms and carried her to the bed. "Now, darlin', you're gonna pay for your disobedience."

Anticipation sent shivers down her back while she faked like she didn't understand what he meant. "Disobedience? When did I disobey you?

"Maybe I should say 'impertinence'," he replied, laying her face up on the bed and then pulling out his bull rope—from where, she didn't know.

"What are you gonna do with that?" she asked, her body humming with the images flashing through her mind.

Without answering, he wrapped it around her wrists in a knot he knew she couldn't pull free from. The next loop secured her to the headboard. "I'm not gonna tie this too tight. It's rough rope, so it will chafe your beautiful wrists if I do." He glanced down and met her gaze with his own scorching look. "Do you trust me?"

She bit her lip for a moment and then nodded.

"I think you'll like this, but you'll have to leave your hands there. You could probably pull free if you wanted to."

The soft slide of his lips from her mouth to her breasts and then lower made her whimper. Breathing got more difficult the closer he got to her pussy. Unable to stop herself, she spread her thighs, begging for his tongue in soft sighs. "Please, Beau."

"I'll take care of you, darlin'."

His shoulders kept her spread as he settled himself between her legs and started licking every inch of her pussy—from her slit up and over her clit, down the outside lips of her pussy.

The torture continued until she'd climaxed at least six times. "I can't stand it anymore, Beau. Pleaseeee. I need you inside me."

The word no more than left her lips and he was there, buried inside her to the hilt.

"Beau!" she screamed, climaxing again.

"Easy, darlin'," he soothed, starting the slow glide of his cock in and out. His lips danced over her face, along her jaw, to her ear, and then across her shoulder. "God, I love bein' inside you. One day soon though, I want your ass. I need to feel those slick muscles tighten around me."

"Fuck me, Beau. I need it hard."

He lifted his chest from hers, braced his arms on the bed next to her, and snapped his hips, driving his cock into her depths until she thought for sure he'd stolen her heart. The fast pace of his thrusts threw her into another climax as he tipped his hips up and slammed into her sweet spot with every plunge.

"Ah, God!"

The low growl and hefty grunts signaled his own climax as he followed her over the precipice of sensual release and into the relaxation of both mind and body.

Their bathtub escapades and being tied to the bed thoroughly exhausted her—to the point she never heard Brandon return and slept like a dead person for the rest of the night, curled into Beau's warm body with her head on his chest.

Morning light streamed through the blinds on the window of the hotel room, dragging Emma from the most delicious dreams of Brandon and Beau making love to her. She rolled onto her side and stretched her hand out across the bed only to find it cold and empty. Her eyes flew open and she sat bolt upright in the bed, glancing around to find Beau. Now the room was quiet—too quiet. Wrapping the sheet around her body, she slid out of the bed and walked into the living room of the suite. Brandon sat sipping coffee while he read the paper. Beau was nowhere to be found.

Brandon glanced up and smiled. "Mornin', honey."

"Where's Beau?"

"Gone for the day." He patted the seat on the couch next to him. "Sit with me. Would you like coffee?"

"Yes, please," she replied, tugging the sheet higher. Why, she didn't know. It wasn't like Brandon hadn't already seen everything she had to offer.

"Cream and sugar?"

"Yeah, thanks"

He handed her the cup, and she took two healthy swallows before she set it back on the table.

"I'm assuming since you're here and he's not, it's your day to spend with me."

"Yes." His eyes twinkled with mischief, and she squirmed on the seat wondering what he planned. It would be nice to get to know Brandon a little more outside of his country music star persona.

"So what's the plan?"

"Nothin' too huge. I want you to show me your life."

Her heart began to pound and her palms started to sweat at his suggestion. *This is so personal. I wonder what brought this on.* "My life? I don't understand."

With both of his hands grasping hers, he said, "Show me Emma Weston. I want to know everything about you. Show me where you went to school, show me your parents' place on horseback, introduce me to some of your friends—things like that."

"Why?" she asked, her thoughts skipping off into unknown territory. Why he wanted to know so much about her made her nervous and excited at the same time.

"Because you're special. You're bright, funny, sexy, charming, sexy—"

A small laugh spilled from her lips. "You said that twice."

"I know, but what can I say? You're a very beautiful woman."

"Okay, Mr. Charm-The-Panties-Off-A-Girl stud muffin. I'm sure you say those words to every woman you meet."

A frown wrinkled the skin between his dark eyebrows. "Not really."

She snorted and covered her mouth.

"I confess to charming the ladies, yes, but I don't say things if I don't mean them." He lifted her hands to his mouth and sucked her index finger between his lips.

Desire zinged straight to her pussy, and her body went from cool and collected to hot and needy in a flash.

When he finally released her from his spell, he said, "I see you brought a change of clothes."

"Yes."

"Why don't you take a shower, and I'll call for room service to bring us something to eat." With her hand in his, he helped her to her feet and turned her toward the bathroom. "I may join you in a few moments." The heat of his whispered words against her ear sent shivers down her spine. His small laugh warmed her skin, and his lips did amazing things to her neck as he slid them over her bare shoulder.

A gentle push to her backside propelled her toward the bathroom, while the heat in his eyes when she glanced over her shoulder promised delights to come. The thought of shower sex with Brandon had her pressing her thighs together, hoping to relieve even a little of the pressure building.

After she closed the door, she dropped the sheet to the floor and moved toward the handles. The massive stall had several jets and a rain-type head, and when she turned the tap on, water shot from every direction. The hot spray pounded into her flesh in a rhythmic cadence, relaxing the bunched muscles of her shoulders and back. Tension uncoiled slowly as she dropped her head forward, closed her eyes and sighed. Really, she didn't have a reason to be so tense, especially after the mind-blowing sex with Beau the night before.

Today Brandon had the chance to wine and dine her, and she couldn't wait to see what he planned. He wanted to know her—the real her—and the thought intrigued her.

Her surprised squeak echoed in the tile stall when Brandon took her left nipple in his mouth. She hadn't heard him come into the bathroom. "You scared me."

The wicked lap of his tongue over the aroused tip made her moan softly and clasp his head harder against her chest. The slow crawl of his fingers up the inside of her leg felt deliciously sexy, and she widened her stance, silently begging for more, but he avoided her needy core. His warm mouth closed over the right nipple and she whimpered. One fingertip brushed her clit, bringing her body to the edge of climax in seconds. God, these two know exactly what to do to push her to the top and hold her there.

"Please, Brandon. Touch me," she begged, thrusting her hips forward encouraging him to spear his fingers into her pussy.

"I'm gonna do more than touch you, honey. I plan to fuck you against the wall in this stall. I want to pound into your pussy until we're both screaming loud enough to rattle the windows." Without any other preamble, he grabbed her by the waist, braced her back against the cold tile shower, and lifted her legs around his waist. "Sorry, honey. I know the tile's cold."

"Damn," she hissed and then groaned. "I love when you're forceful. It's hotter than hell."

The tip of his bare cock nudged at her opening, seeking entrance into her needy, pulsating pussy. "Fuck me, Brandon. I want it all."

"No condom?"

Her gaze caught his, searching for anything to tell her if she could trust him with her body like she trusted him with her heart. "I'm clean and on the pill."

He braced his forehead against hers and said, "I've always insisted on a condom, but with you, I need to feel your pussy without anything between us. I want to feel every ripple, every spasm, every greedy squeeze."

"Such a sexy, smooth talker." She pushed her bottom down, teasing herself with the initial penetration of the head of his cock. "All the way, Brandon. Every inch, baby."

With one deep thrust, he buried himself inside her to the balls. "Oh yeah," he moaned. "Perfect."

"Yes, yes, yes."

The slow, rhythmic push of his cock felt fantastic, but she wanted more—so much more. A soft whimper escaped her mouth as she buried her face against his neck. "Harder."

"I can't, Emma. I'll explode."

"We can do it again. Harder, Brandon. Fuck me hard."

He inhaled sharply and picked up his pace until he was pounding away at her flesh. Every thrust of his hips brought her closer to ignition. She dug her fingernails into his shoulders and nipped at the side of his neck.

"Next time I want your ass, honey. God, you have such a fantastic ass."

His dirty talk and the anticipation of feeling his cock deep in her ass again had her screaming his name as her climax washed over her like a rogue wave against the sand. Her whole body tingled and flushed with heat while Brandon continued stroking his cock in and out of her pussy.

His rapid, harsh panting and clenched jaw told her he hung on the edge.

"Come for me, Brandon. I want to feel all that luscious cream you're hiding splash the inside of my pussy."

"Holy hell," he growled, losing the hold on his pleasure and squirting cum deep inside her.

Chapter Twelve

Montana summer heat beat down on their heads as they rode east across the plains of her father's land. Wildflowers bloomed around them in a multitude of colors ranging from reds to purples and oranges. The mountains looming in the distance looked close enough to touch as the mid-day sun heated the entire area. Montana could go from hotter than Hades to cool and inviting during the summer months.

"Your dad owns all this?" he asked, glancing at the beauty riding next to him. God, she looked fantastic with the wind blowing in her hair, the twinkle in her blue eyes, and the wide smile on her lips.

"Yep. He has fifteen thousand acres, give or take. This land has been in my family for generations. My great-great-grandfather settled here back when there wasn't much in the state except for wide open spaces."

"I love Montana," he replied, thinking about the many summers he'd spent on his parents' place riding alongside Beau, the power of the horse beneath him and the wind ruffling his hair. Lately he'd realized how much he'd missed being able to kick back and forget the country star thing for a while. The horses moved along at a slow, steady pace, making it easy to talk.

"You are technically from here, right?" Emma asked. "Montana, I mean."

"Yeah. My parents still have a place out east of the mountains. They breed horses and cattle."

"Sweet."

He didn't discuss his youth much, especially with women. Most of the time, he fucked 'em and disappeared so fast, they never knew what had hit them...but not Emma. He wanted to share his life—his past with the one woman who'd penetrated the shell he'd erected around his heart.

"Beau told me about your sister. I'm sorry. I can't imagine what it's like to lose a sibling."

He didn't reply right away. Anger rushed through him for a moment when he thought about Beau sharing Bailey like that. They'd agreed years ago to keep her to themselves, so they could cherish her memory without revealing her problems to the world. Yeah, he'd told the crowd about her during the concert, but he didn't want to share the other medical issues she had. Bailey was special, and he'd wanted to continue to hold her close to his heart without hearing the pity in people's words.

"What's wrong?"

"Nothin'."

Reining her horse to a stop, she waited for him to follow suit. "Are you angry he told me?"

The compassion and sorrow shining in her eyes broke down the barriers of his emotions. "At first, yeah, but not now. It seems natural to share her with you. Did he tell you she was a triplet?"

"Yeah. I can tell she meant a lot to both of you, and I'm sure you wished you could have protected her from everything."

"I did. I do." He raked his fingers through his hair and stared off into the distance. "She meant everything to us."

Emma took his hand and squeezed his fingers.

"Thanks for listening. It's hard for me to talk about it."

She glanced around and nodded to some shade trees in the distance. "How about we get our picnic set up over there?"

"Sounds good." He cocked his head to the side. "Race you!"

The pounding of hooves drifted off into the vast grassy prairie as he pushed his horse into a faster pace. *Damn, the girl can ride.* Neck in neck, they sped across the prairie toward the grove of trees. Her laugher reached his ears and he couldn't help but smile. This was Emma in her element, and he couldn't help loving this woman who met life head on, grabbed it by the horns, and rode it like a bucking bull.

As they skidded to a halt, their horses breathing hard, he jumped off and swept her up in a tight hug, swinging her around in a circle. Her laughter made every worry disappear, and he wanted to hear it day after day for the rest of their lives. *God, I'm pathetic.*

"I'm hungry. How about we break out our lunch and sit under the tree?"

She kissed his lips quickly and said, "Good plan, but you'll have to let me go so I can get the stuff out of the pack."

Her lips called to him to taste, long and slow, exploring her mouth with his tongue and revving up the heat. Their tongues danced from her mouth to his and back, sliding over each other as he savored her soft sighs and whispered moans.

"Lordy, Emma. I could kiss you all day," he murmured, resting his forehead against hers.

"Me, too, Brandon. You're one damned good kisser."

"Who's better? Me or Beau?"

She stepped back and laughed. "Oh, I'm so not goin' there, mister. You don't need any more ego stroking and I refuse to play into the natural competition you two seem to have over everythin'."

Minutes later, the blanket lay across the soft grass, and Emma retrieved the picnic from her saddle bag.

"We have ham sandwiches, potato salad, sweet tea, and chips," she said, handing him a paper plate with all the various ingredients of their picnic. "I made the sandwiches, but my dad's kitchen helper, Gabrielle, made the potato salad. She's more of a cook, housekeeper, and all around keep-everyone-in-line kind of person.

"Do you cook much?"

"Sometimes," she replied, sliding the fork between her lips. "I have the basics down, I think, but I'm not much of a cookin' from scratch sort of gal. My mom, and then Gabrielle, tried to teach me, but I can't seem to get it right."

"More practice, maybe?"

She shrugged and stared at her plate. "Maybe. I never seem to have time to spend hours in the kitchen. I'd rather be out in the barn with the animals, ridin' across the fields out here, mendin' fences—you know."

"Cowboy stuff," they said in unison and laughed.

"I know the feeling, Emma. Sometimes I wish I could go back to the simpler days before all the craziness of tourin' and singin'."

"Don't you like singin'?"

"I love it, but it would be nice to be able to go to the store without someone I don't know recognizing me. You can't imagine how hard it is to take a lady out on a date and get interrupted a dozen times for pictures and autographs. Privacy would be great. Sometimes this star stuff isn't all it's cracked up to be. I'm sure Beau gets it, too."

"But you've been singin' since you were small."

He glanced across the fields they'd ridden through and sighed. "Do you have any idea what it's like never to know if a woman is after you or your money?"

"Can't say that I do, since I don't do women," she replied with a little grin.

His laugh came out as a small snort.

"How do you know I'm not after your money, Brandon?" she asked, lying on her side on the blanket and propping herself up on her hand. "What if I'm some money-crazed fangirl who wants to trap you and Beau into a relationship?"

"Because for some unknown reason, I trust you, Emma." He stretched out beside her and tugged her over so she lay completely on top of him. "Mmm. I like this position. Ready for a ride, cowgirl?"

"I thought you said the next time you were gonna take my ass, big boy."

Need speared right to his cock the moment her words left her mouth. He loved anal sex, and when he'd been in her ass before, it felt perfect—better than anything he'd experienced before. Unable to stop himself, the flat of his palm came down on her ass. "Saucy wench. Strip."

Jumping to her feet, she whipped her shirt over her head, taking her sports bra with it, and then pushed her jeans and underwear off her feet. "You're still dressed."

"Yep, and I'm gonna stay that way," he replied, sitting up to crouch on his knees.

"Then how are you gonna fuck me?"

"You'll see. On your hands and knees, baby doll, and spread your ass cheeks for me." When she'd done what he asked, he sucked in a ragged breath and leaned over to kiss her butt cheeks. "What a sight you are, Emma, honey. I could fuck you until the end of time, just like this." The rasp of his zipper in the afternoon air sounded loud to him, and he glanced around to make sure they were alone. The last thing he wanted on this earth was for Emma to be embarrassed about being with him. He shoved his jeans and boxers down around his knees, releasing his cock and balls from their confines. Grabbing the condom from his front pocket and the small tube of lube he'd brought, he made everything—including her puckered hole—slick and ready.

"Hurry, Brandon," she whispered, wiggling her butt, encouraging him with every movement.

God, she made him hotter than hell with her begging words. He penetrated her hole with two fingers and stretched her well before he did anything else. The last thing he wanted was pain for his girl. His girl. He liked the sound of that.

"Ready?"

"Oh yeah," she whispered, pushing back against his fingers. "Fill me up, cowboy."

The slow penetration of his cock into her ass felt like heaven and hell. The slick walls of her ass gripped him tight as he slowly pushed into her tight passage. "Relax and let me in, Emma."

"I'm trying. It burns a bit."

"I know, honey. Inhale and then exhale slowly."

Doing what he asked, her whole body relaxed on the exhale, and he pushed the rest of his cock deep inside her. "Fuck, you're amazing."

"Oh yeah. Perfect. You feel so good," she whispered, dropping her head down on her folded arms, which raised her ass higher.

A groan left his mouth when she pushed back and squeezed him with her muscles. "You okay?" he asked.

"Fantastic, but Brandon?"

"Yeah?"

"You need to move. I can't stand it anymore. I need you to fuck me hard."

"With pleasure," he growled, pulling his cock almost all the way out before slowly sliding it back in. "I wish I had a toy here. I'd shove it inside your pretty pussy and fuck your ass at the same time."

"Next time we'll play with toys."

"Next time," he repeated, shoving his cock in and out of her, loving her willingness to experiment.

Her anal muscles held him tight enough, he wasn't sure he could hold off his climax if she didn't hurry and come along. Needing to make her lose control, he found her clit with his fingers and started stroking until it hardened more under his touch. High-pitched whimpers left her mouth, and her hips bucked while he continued to pound into her, increasing the pace of his thrusts until he felt her climax building.

"Come for me, sweetheart. Come for me."

An explosive climax shook her frame, and she screamed loud enough, they probably heard her in the next county, but he didn't care. He'd made Emma feel good, and nothing else mattered. With her muscles spasming around his cock, he couldn't forestall his own climax any longer. The blood roared in his ears, and his body trembled from the force of it.

When his vision cleared and he could move again, he pulled out of her ass and collapsed on the ground beside her. "God, you're amazing."

"Glad you liked it," she said with a small giggle. "I aim to please, and believe me, you aren't easy to please."

"Why do you say that?" he asked, worried she felt she couldn't continue to please him as he tugged his boxers and jeans back up.

"How many women have you slept with in the last year?"

He frowned and thought back to the mindless, nameless hoard of women he'd slept with. "To tell you the truth, I don't know."

"And if you'd found one who pleased you outside of ridin' your dick, don't you think you might have wanted to see her again?"

"Maybe, but I haven't really...until now. I did have one serious relationship, or what I thought was serious until I realized she only wanted the money." Her hair felt like spun silk between his fingers as he brushed the curls back behind her ear. "I can't seem to get enough of you."

"What happens after you leave? I mean, the bus should be fixed soon, and you and Beau will be off to God only knows where."

"I don't know, Emma. I wish I did. I'm sure we can work out somethin'. I haven't gotten my fill of you yet." The thought of leaving Emma behind soured his stomach.

The jingle of his cell phone cut through the tight atmosphere developing between them. He cussed out loud when he saw Beau's name on the caller ID.

"What?" he snapped when he opened his phone. "This is my time with Emma. What's so important—"

"Brandon you need to come to the room. We have a problem."

"Can't it wait? We're out ridin'."

"No. It's your management company. You need to be here to hear this. I won't go into it on the phone." The tone of Beau's voice and the evasive answers worried Brandon. It wasn't like Beau to get upset about anything.

"All right. We'll ride back to Emma's dad's place, but it's going to be a couple of hours before we get back and drive into town."

"Its fine, but we need to take care of this soon."

Brandon snapped the phone shut and stood. "We need to get back. Beau says there's a problem of some sort, and I need to be there."

"Okay," she replied, pulling her clothes back on.

Their picnic lunch ended up stuffed back into the saddle bags.

* * * *

They made the ride back to the house in complete and stifling silence. Emma didn't know what to make of Brandon's mood. He'd been so playful and loving out on their picnic, she could almost believe he cared about her.

Deciding to broach the subject once they'd returned to the barn, she said, "Brandon?"

"Yeah?"

"I hope it's nothin' serious."

He glanced over at her from where he stood brushing down his horse. "Me, too, honey, but Beau sounded worried."

"Don't you two have the twin thing where you can feel each others' moods and stuff? I've heard of it before between twins."

"Sometimes, but we usually have to be fairly close to each other. Not like it works miles apart," he replied, finishing up and leading the gelding into his stall. "Are you about ready to go?"

"Yeah. Just let me put Missy away. Can you drop her tack in the storeroom for me along with yours?"

"Sure, honey."

Several moments later, they bounced down the dirt driveway of her dad's place, heading back to town in her truck. A bad feeling sat like a lump of coal in her belly. For some reason, she knew somethin' bad was gonna happen, and she tried to brace herself for it.

The front of the hotel came into view about fifteen minutes later, and she steeled her heart for whatever news Beau had to share. The walk up to their suite felt like what she thought it might be like to walk death row. Trepidation rolled down her spine and made her tremble with uncertainty.

"It'll be fine, honey," Brandon said, taking her hand in his and kissing her fingertips.

"I don't know, Brandon. I have a bad feelin' about this."

Brandon slipped his key card into the door and pushed it open. "Beau?"

"In here," Beau replied from the direction of the dining room area. "You might as well grab a drink, brother, you aren't gonna like this."

When they rounded the corner of the living room and Brandon headed for the bar, Beau looked surprised to see her. "Emma?"

"Hey."

"Hi. I didn't realize Brandon was bringing you along," he replied, brushing her lips with his. "Did you enjoy your day?"

"Yeah. We went ridin' and had a picnic."

"Sounds like fun." The look in his eyes worried her. He looked tired, torn and pissed off.

Deciding she'd rather not hear this now that she was faced with whatever bad news this entailed, she said, "I need to use the little girls' room, guys. I'll be back in a minute." She pushed the bathroom door open and then shut it behind her. It only took seconds for the raised tones to penetrate the door. Even though they shouted, she couldn't make out the words clearly, but anger and irritation rang in their voices.

Moments later silence filled the suite, and she figured she needed to go back out there. Hopefully everything had blown over. When she walked back into the living room, she could see Beau standing by the bay windows, looking out over the wildflowers and the mountains in the distance, and Brandon sitting in the chair, tapping his fingers against the leather.

"Guys?"

"Emma, honey," Brandon said, getting to his feet. "Come here."

She moved into his embrace and let him hug her tight. The trembling of his body as he held her scared her more than anything. "What's wrong? What's happened?"

"Nothin' for you to worry your pretty head about," Brandon answered.

"Bullshit, Brandon. She has the right to know," Beau snapped.

"Know what? You're scaring me."

Brandon glared at Beau for a moment and then sighed. "Sit down, Emma. We need to talk to you."

The ending of their little love affair had always loomed in the dark corners, just waiting to rear its ugly head and force her to face the fact of their departure. The tightness around Beau's mouth and the anger floating in Brandon's eyes made her realize the end was closer than she'd thought.

"Now, what's this all about?"

"God, I hate this!" Beau shouted. "Tell them no, Brandon. Tell them we have something we need to finish here."

"We've been over this, Beau. I can't and neither can you. They could cancel my contract, and I'd be out on my ear. There's no room for a difficult-to-deal-with performer in country music. You know that! You've been pounding it into my head for the last five years."

"Damn it! This isn't fair."

"Uh…would someone please explain?" Emma asked.

Brandon dropped onto the couch next to her and took her hand in his. "We have to leave."

"I know. When the bus is finished being repaired—"

"No, honey, now. Today."

"What? No, you can't leave yet." *I'm not ready for them to leave.*

"I know, Emma. God, I know," he said, raking his fingers through his hair. "Neither of us wants to leave, but we have to. My management company called earlier, while we were out. They're sending a private jet to pick us up to fly us back to Nashville. They've set up another bus to get us around until ours is fixed."

"I thought you'd cancelled the shows you had coming up," she said, her gaze meeting Brandon's, hoping beyond hope this wasn't real. They couldn't be leaving so soon.

"I called them and told them to," Beau interjected, his own despair and disbelief written on his face as he sat down on her other side and gathered her into his arms. "But apparently they didn't. They've decided to make other arrangements for Brandon to be there, and I have to go with him."

Tears burned her eyes, and one trickled down her cheek. This couldn't be happening. They can't leave yet.

"I'm sorry, Emma," Beau whispered, wiping the tear from her cheek. "I wish we had more time."

Brandon rose to his feet and began to pace back and forth. "I know. Come with us, Emma."

"What?" she asked, pulling away from Beau. "I can't. I have a life here. School. My family."

"You can leave that. This would be us. You, me and Beau. We'll take care of you. I have more than enough money. Beau can tell you."

"It's not about the money, Brandon. It's not about you and Beau. This is me. I can't up and leave everything I know."

Beau's eyes were shadowed with hurt and indecision. "Brandon, we can't do this to her. It's not fair to make her chose."

"I care about you, both of you, but I won't leave my family, my friends, or my life here." She got to her feet and backed up.

"Emma, please," Brandon said, taking her hands. "I think I'm falling in love with you. I need you with me—with both of us. I know Beau feels the same."

Disbelief, elation, and then disappointment tore at her heart. "Don't, Brandon. I can't handle it. Please." She pulled away and glanced at Beau, then back to Brandon. "I guess this is good-bye then." Unable to stop herself from one last touch, she pressed her lips to Brandon's and then to Beau's. "Please don't hate me."

"I could never hate you, darlin'," Beau said, running his hand down her back.

"Me either. You know how to get in touch with us if you want to, right?" Brandon added.

"No, but it's probably best." She closed her eyes and bit her lip. "I…need to move on. It's been great, and I'll never forget either of you, but—" With her knuckle pressed against her lips to stop the choking sobs, she grabbed her purse and rushed out the door.

Chapter Thirteen

Four months. Four fucking months since either of them had seen or talked to Emma and it was driving Beau absolutely insane. At the moment, they sat in one of the houses Brandon owned, in a suburb of Nashville. When he'd made it big, Brandon had said he wanted to own a home with some acreage. Nashville seemed the logical place, with all the time he had to spend in the studios. Right now, all Beau wanted to do was see Emma. She refused to answer their phone calls, and every avenue they'd tried got shut down by those around her.

Beau paced the living room, stopping every so often to glance out at the barren landscape. The pastures behind the house stretched for miles over the gentle slope of the terrain. Horses moved in and out of the corrals, hunting for morsels of hay left from this morning's feeding. "I need to see her, Brandon. I can't stop thinkin' about her."

"I know, Beau. I feel the same way, but we're booked solid on this tour for another month. You know traveling to Montana in the fuckin' dead of winter is a bad idea."

"I know." He slammed his fist down on the tabletop under the window and cussed when the skin on his knuckles broke and bled. "Son of a bitch! I can't sleep. I can't eat. I sure as hell can't fuck another woman, and I'm about to lose my mind." Grabbing a paper towel from the kitchen, he wrapped his knuckles to stop the bleeding and glanced at his brother. "Where's the number you found? I'm gonna try callin' her again."

"She's not takin' our calls, Beau. We've tried this how many times now?"

"I don't care. I need to hear her voice, even if it's just the voicemail." He sank down on the couch, laying his head against the back. "I never thought I'd find the woman I want to spend the rest of my life with by gettin' into a car accident. How in the hell did I fall in love with her?"

"I wish I knew," Brandon whispered, his voice soft and in awe. "If I had the answer to that, I wouldn't be feelin' the same way. I love her too, and it's drivin' me nuts not talking to her or being near her. We should never have left Red Rock without telling her how we felt."

"If those assholes from Nelson and Britchert hadn't corralled us onto the plane so damned fast, I would have. Hell, we were going after her when they caught us in the lobby. This is such a fuckin' mess. Callin' her house didn't work—her dad refused to tell her we called. Cade won't talk to us either."

"Do you blame them? They think we left her high and dry. Have you tried callin' her friend Becky? Maybe she can tell us how Emma is, at least."

Beau snapped his fingers and sat up. He grabbed his phone and dialed information for Red Rock. When he had Becky's number, he crossed his fingers and dialed.

"Hello?"

"Becky?"

"Yes, who is this?"

"It's Beau Tucker. Don't hang up please. I need to talk to you."

"Well, I don't want to talk to you, you asshole, or your brother, either. How in the hell could you leave Emma like that?" she snarled into the phone. "You're both fucking worthless pieces of shit, and I hope your nuts fall off."

The phone clicked in his ear. "Damn it! Is the whole goddamn town pissed at us?" Frustration and fear raced through his mind. What if they never got to see her again? What if he never held her again?

"Probably," Brandon replied. "But I have one more idea. Didn't you say you met Emma's gram when you went out to dinner with her?"

"Yeah, but she basically threatened to haunt us for the next hundred years if we hurt Emma. She's probably put a spell or something on us already."

"Call her. I think she'll listen," Brandon said. He lifted a beer bottle to his lips.

"You didn't even meet her, Brandon. How would you know?"

"Just a gut feeling."

"Fine," Beau growled, dialing information again. Thank goodness Emma had mentioned her grandmother's real name after their conversation at the restaurant. His gut felt like a rock as he punched in the phone number.

"Hello?"

"Mrs. Oliver?" he asked, hope filling his heart.

"Yes? Who is this?"

"It's Beau Tucker. I met you at the restaurant in Watertown, the night Emma and I went to dinner. Do you remember me?"

"I'd say so son. I hope you aren't back in Red Rock. I wouldn't be surprised if there wasn't a bounty on your head for leavin' the way you did. Want to explain it to me before I come after you with my shotgun?"

His heart started to hammer for the first time since they'd left Red Rock. "Yes ma'am, I do. You see, I had called Brandon's management company and cancelled the shows he had coming up for a few weeks in order to have time with Emma and give the garage time to fix his bus. His management company took matters into their own hands and sent someone out to Red Rock to fetch us home like a couple of wayward children. We didn't have much choice but to leave, or they could have cancelled Brandon's recording contract."

"You know you hurt her, right?"

"Yes ma'am, and we aim to make it right."

"Oh? How do you plan to do that?"

Beau's heart sank. Her gram was their only hope, and she didn't sound too forgiving either. "We aren't sure, really. She won't take our calls, Becky hung up on us, her dad and Cade won't talk to us…"

"Do you blame them?" the woman asked. "She's been a mess since you two skipped town."

"No, I sure don't, but we can't explain if no one will talk to us."

"I'm listening, son, so spill it. I ain't got all day." Silence enveloped the phone line as he tried to think of what else to say. "Do you love her?"

"Yes ma'am, and so does my brother." Hope raced through him. At least her gram had given him a chance to explain. "He's standing here next to me, nodding like a crazy fool."

A bubbly chuckle met his ear, and he smiled for the first time since Emma had run out the door, taking his heart with her.

"Did you tell her?"

"No ma'am, but we want to rectify the situation."

"Then I suggest you high-tail your asses back out here and tell her."

"It's not quite so simple. Brandon has another month of touring to do before he can take any time off and—"

"I'll ask this again, son. Do you love her?"

Beau sat in silence for several moments until the light bulb went on in his head. "We'll be there tomorrow mornin' ma'am."

"That's what I wanted to hear, son." Mrs. Oliver rattled off her address and said, "Come by here when you get off the plane. I'll get her over here where you can talk to her privately, without her family and friends hovering. She hasn't spent much time alone the last couple of months, I'll warn you of that now. She's even been datin', although no one I want her tied to. You boys are special, and even though I never got a chance to meet your twin, if he's like you, you'll both make a damned nice addition to the family."

"Thank you, Mrs. Oliver. You're a doll!"

"No thankin' me until you get things situated with Emma. I'm not guaranteein' she'll listen when she does see you both, but I know she's been miserable since you left. Now I'll let you go, since you've got plans to make, and I'll see you tomorrow."

The phone clicked in his ear, and he turned to Brandon with a smile he knew about split his face.

"So, what did she say?"

"We're goin' to Red Rock tomorrow."

"What the fuck?" Brandon's eyes were wide and disbelieving as he turned back toward Beau from his pacing of the living room. "We can't get there from here in one day, Beau. Are you nuts?"

"No. We're using some of your hard-earned money, Brandon. We're flying there, and I don't care if we have to rent a private plane—we are going to Red Rock to see Emma."

* * * *

Emma drove down the snow-covered streets of Red Rock toward Gram Oliver's house. Christmas was fast approaching, and Gram had asked for help with the baking and decorating she did for the local hospital every year. Today they planned to bake cookies and make candy.

Her radio blared country music, and she tapped her fingers to the beat of a new song. She hadn't heard it before, but she knew the voice—she listened to it every night on her cell phone before she went to bed. She still had every message they'd ever left her on her voicemail. No, she couldn't talk to them, but she could listen to their words and pretend they loved her like she loved them. It helped—God knew why, but it did. She knew they'd had to go, and she really couldn't blame them for how everything went down during the last day she'd seen them this summer.

Her friends and family, however, blamed them for everything, and she hoped they'd never set foot in Red Rock again—they might not leave here alive. Kale and Laurel had threatened to lock them up and throw away the key. Cade and Natalie wanted them dead. Becky and Seth wanted to castrate them both. And her dad?

Oh, Lord. If he ever got hold of them, not only would they not leave here alive, he'd bury them somewhere in the middle of his pasture, and no one would ever find the bodies.

But Gram, God bless her soul, understood. She never said a word about Beau and Brandon the day Emma came over and cried until her heart felt lighter and she could actually say their names without breaking down. Gram understood she loved the two stubborn men, but she also knew Emma couldn't leave Red Rock.

Or so she'd thought. Since Beau and Brandon left, she'd done some thinkin'. Being with them meant everything to her. They were her other two-thirds. The two of them together completed her, and she'd made plans to fly out to Nashville next week and get the whole thing out in the open. She had to. She couldn't continue this way. Her plan had holes, yes, but she didn't know what else to do except talk to them and find out their true feelings. Did they love her like she loved them? Did they want her to be a permanent part of their lives? Those questions needed answers, and the only way she knew how to get them was to be in their faces.

Gram's house came into view, and Emma smiled. Grandmother Oliver always went all-out when it came to Christmas, and this year was no exception. She had various inflatable ornaments scattered across her lawn. Twinkling lights surrounded every window and the eaves of the house, and Emma wondered who'd put them up there. "Probably Cade." A huge Christmas tree filled the whole front window of the house with its colored lights and accoutrement of ornaments from sixty-eight years of marriage to Doctor Oliver.

Emma pulled into the driveway and shut the engine on her truck off as she stared at the brightly lit house.

Someday she wanted her own house, with a loving husband and a passel of kids. Unfortunately, at the moment, there were only two men she could imagine her life with, and she still needed to work things out with them. "Soon. Next week I'll get this all straightened out one way or another. Either they'll declare their love for me, or I'll never see them again." Her heart cracked at the thought. It had only been four months, and she could barely function from day to day. The emptiness and loneliness wouldn't go away.

She grabbed her groceries and struggled out of the truck, slamming the door shut with her leg and almost losing her footing on the slippery driveway. "Cade needs to get over here and shovel this driveway before Gram breaks a hip or somethin'."

Emma looked up to find Gram standing on the covered porch, her shawl around her frail shoulders, calling out, "Emma, quit talking to yourself, child, and get in here where it's warm. Damn, I'd swear it's fifty below out there."

After she stepped up onto the porch, Gram ushered her through the front door and quickly closed it behind them.

"Not quite, Gram, but close." Emma set the bags on the dining room table and leaned down slightly to kiss Gram's cheeks. "At least it's warm in the house."

"Did you bring everything I asked you to bring?"

"Yes'm, but I'm a bit confused why you wanted the duct tape?"

"Oh, somethin' I think might require it. Nothing huge, but I wanted to make sure I had some in case."

Emma shrugged and started unloading the bags of groceries. "We're having dinner here, right Gram? I thought since we'd be baking all day, we could order some pizza for dinner."

"Fine by me, honey, but make sure you order, like, four larges."

"You and I can't eat that much pizza." Emma looked at Gram and wondered what was going on. *Has Gram lost her mind? Maybe a little dementia going on here?*

"Uh...well, I want some for leftovers. You know I love cold pizza. And Cade will be bringing Alan over tomorrow afternoon so he and Natalie can go Christmas shopping for him." Gram pulled out her recipe cards and spread them out on the countertop. "Why don't you do the fudge and divinity, and I'll work on the cookie dough."

Emma chuckled and grabbed the two cards she needed. The ingredients were simple enough, but she wasn't much of a baker. "You just want to eat the dough."

The two of them worked side by side for two hours, but Emma noticed how Gram kept watching the clock, sometimes walking to the front of the house to peer outside. "Are you expecting someone, Gram? You seem awful nervous."

"Nope. Not me. I wasn't sure whether Cade and Natalie might come over. I invited Natalie to help us bake this afternoon, but she wasn't sure if she'd have time. She had a fundraiser to go to this afternoon."

The sun began to set behind the mountains as evening approached. It always got dark so early during the winter, it got depressing sometimes. Christmas music played softly in the background while they baked and chatted.

"Have you ever had a chance to talk to those two men you were seeing this summer?"

"Beau and Brandon Tucker?"

"Yes."

Emma bit her lip and sighed. "No, Gram, I haven't. In fact, I've been avoiding their calls since they left."

"Why, Emma? I thought you had feelin's for them?"

"I do, but I know they did what they had to do this past summer, and I wasn't sure if they cared about me enough to want me in their lives. Neither of them ever said they loved me," she said, stirring the batter for brownies.

"Do you love either of them?"

Emma set the bowl down and stretched her back. "Yes, Gram. In fact, I'm in love with both of them. Don't tell Dad or Cade, but I'm going to fly out to Nashville next week so I can talk to them. We need to clear the air, and the only way I can do that is to see them."

A quirky little smile lifted the corners of Gram's mouth, and her eyes twinkled mischievously. "I think you're doing the right thing, honey."

"Thanks." She hugged Gram and then went back to stirring the batter.

The doorbell rang, and Gram said she'd get it, while Emma spread the chocolate batter into the baking dish. Low voices reached her ear as whoever was at the door walked closer to the kitchen with her grandmother.

"Emma, honey. Can you come into the living room, please?"

She shrugged and said, "Be right there, Gram. I'm putting the brownies in."

Once the oven was set and the timer on, she washed her sticky hands and dried them on the spare dish towel sitting on the counter. The black apron she'd put on over her clothes had flour and batter all over it, so she slipped it off and laid it on the table.

The murmur of voices got louder, and she slowed her steps when she heard her name. Could it be Cade and Natalie? Gram had said they might be coming by. When she cleared the corner and saw who sat on the couch with Gram, her breath caught in her throat. She closed her eyes tightly and reopened them. Nope, nothing changed.

Beau and Brandon flanked Gram, who sat between them wearing a shit-eating grin. *No, no, no! I'm not ready for this.*

She spun on her heels and raced for the back door, stepping out onto Gram's patio. Snow swirled and blew across her face. Shivers rolled over her arms, but she wasn't sure if they were from the cold or Beau and Brandon's appearance.

The door slid open behind her, and she tried to decide what to do, her gaze darting back and forth.

"Emma? Come inside, darlin'. It's too fuckin' cold out there, and you don't even have a coat on," Beau said, taking a couple of steps toward her.

"I…" She shook her head and took two more steps into the blowing snow, but he was right there with her.

"Come inside," he whispered, taking her hand and drawing her toward the door.

Taking a fortifying breath, she allowed Beau to lead her into the house and toward the living room. Gram had disappeared, and Brandon stood near the fireplace, which crackled and popped with a cheery fire.

Beau pulled her down on the couch next to him, and Brandon took the other side. Each held one of her hands and stroked her knuckles.

"What are you doin' here?" she asked, not sure if she wanted to know. *What if they don't love me like I love them?*

Beau said, "We needed to talk to you, darlin', and we both felt the best thing would be to come here and see you."

"Why didn't you answer our calls, Emma?" Brandon asked, pain clearly etched on his face. "We tried several times."

"I know. I have all the voicemails."

"You know? Why didn't you call back or answer?"

Faced with her avoidance over the last several months, uncertainty bloomed in her mind. She didn't know what she'd do if they only wanted her for a few nights of wild sex again. "I…uh…I needed some time to sort everythin' out."

"Is it sorted now?" Beau asked.

"To some degree, yes, I think so—but how did you get time to come here? You had a month left on this tour."

"I still do," Brandon replied, bringing her hand to his mouth and kissing her fingers. "But this is more important. *You're* more important."

Her stomach rolled over, and her heart skipped a beat. "More important than your career?"

"Yes."

Emma sat back against the floral sofa and looked at Brandon and then Beau. "I don't understand."

"We're here because we love you, Emma. You mean everythin' to us, and we don't want to live without you anymore," Beau stated, his eyes serious and pleading.

"You, too?" she said, looking at Brandon.

"Yeah. I love you too, and I want you with me and Beau."

"But your career. What about that?"

"We've got it all worked out, Emma. You'll marry Brandon, and then we'll have a separate ceremony for all three of us. That way all of his assets and money will belong to you should anything ever happen to him."

She looked from one brother to the other twice and then got to her feet. She needed to maintain some distance so she could absorb what was going on here. "Did you just propose to me for Brandon?" she asked Beau.

His warm chuckle sent shivers down her back. God, she'd missed them—everything about them. The easy smiles, the twinkling eyes, the wicked lips. The torturous hands, and especially the daring way they made love to her. "I proposed to you from both of us...but wait, we need to do this right."

Both men got to their feet and walked over to her. Beau went down on his left knee and Brandon went down on his right. Each man pulled a diamond ring from his pocket and held it up in front of her.

"I love you more than life itself, Emma, and I'm askin' you to do me the honor of becomin' my wife." Beau took her left hand. "Please?"

Tears streamed down her cheeks. Never in a million years would she have imagined these two gorgeous men fallin' in love with her, much less askin' her to marry him. "How is it gonna work? We're going to live in a ménage relationship?"

"No one needs to know except our families, Em. It's our business and no one else's," Brandon replied. "No more excuses. Will you marry me?"

"And me?" Beau added.

"Yes, I'll marry you. Both of you," she replied, dropping to her knees in front of them.

Beau slipped his ring on her left ring finger, and then Brandon slipped his onto her right hand. "It'll stay there until we get the wedding ring on. Then we'll move mine to your left hand, too."

"So is there gonna be a weddin' or not?" Gram asked from the doorway to the kitchen. "Or do I need to get the duct tape?"

All three of them laughed, getting to their feet and wrapping Gram in their arms.

"Yes, Gram, there's gonna be a weddin'. Not sure when yet, but there will be," Emma said, kissing her grandmother's cheek and whispering, 'Thank you,' in her ear.

Epilogue

Flashbulbs blinked like streaks of lightning during a summer storm when they stepped from the limousine and out onto the red carpet stretched in front of them. Brandon held her hand and Beau placed his palm on her lower back. Whispers of gossip had surrounded them ever since they brought Emma back to Nashville after the wedding a little over a year ago, and they were rarely seen apart. No one knew for sure they'd made themselves a triad, but the rumor mill always speculated. Tonight, she didn't care what anyone said. She had her men at her sides, and the evening belonged to Brandon. He'd worked his ass off touring, promoting, and changing his image from the happy-go-lucky, partying, spoiled country star to a hard-working family man. The last two singles off his new CD had hit number one, and tonight he was up for several Country Music Association awards, including Entertainer of the Year.

"Brandon!"

Several people yelled, and girls screamed his name over and over. He flashed his million dollar smile and tucked Emma against his side.

A reporter from *Entertainment Tonight* stopped them. "Brandon, can we talk to you for a moment, please?" she asked.

"Sure."

"You've done so well this year. Two number ones already, and this album hasn't even been out six months. It debuted at number two on *Billboard*'s top 200. You've got a beautiful wife and you seem to be riding the golden rainbow. How does it feel?"

"I've been blessed."

Emma's heart swelled with pride at her husband and his accomplishments, but mostly at the love in his eyes.

"What's on the horizon?"

"You mean besides the birth of my child?"

Everyone around them chuckled.

"Well, yes. You've been a busy man lately."

"Yes, I have. Both my brother and I have been extremely busy. He has a successful buckin' bull business goin' on, I've had phenomenal success with this CD, and my beautiful wife is having my child. What more could I ask for?"

"Brandon!" someone yelled, and when Emma glanced toward the railing separating them from the hoards of fans, a smile spread across her face.

"It's Charlene," she whispered against Brandon's ear.

"Get her over here," he snapped to a security guard to his left.

The guard brought Charlene from behind the barricade, and Emma hugged her even though her very pregnant stomach got in the way of a real hug. "You look fabulous, honey. How are you?"

"Good. Momma says the new medicine they have me on is working."

"I hate that you had to move here to be treated."

"It's okay. I kinda like it here."

"Where's your parents, Charlene?" Brandon asked.

The little girl pointed to the right and her parents waved frantically. Brandon and Beau glanced at each other and Beau nodded.

The reporter had moved onto someone else behind them, and the next thing Emma knew, Charlene and her parents stood next to them.

"Tickets?" Brandon asked, in the twin-to-twin thing Emma couldn't possibly understand, even though she lived with these two.

"Right here," Beau replied, pulling them from inside his jacket pocket. "They aren't the best."

"It's fine, son," Charlene's dad said. "We're pleased as punch to be here tonight."

Emma glanced at Brandon and then Beau. "I knew you two were up to somethin', when we were getting dressed."

"Not us," Brandon replied with a wicked grin and a quick kiss to her lips. "I wish your family could come, Emma."

"Its fine, honey," she replied, placing her palm against his cheek. "They support us from afar with our relationship and your career."

"Yes, they do. They've been fabulous."

They made their way inside with the wave of people. Charlene and her parents went toward the stairs leading to the balcony, and she, Brandon, and Beau took the aisle down toward the front, where their seats were. She knew they'd be close, but wow. She never would have imagined being here with all the stars she'd listened to over the years. George Strait, Reba McIntyre, Carrie Underwood, and several others mingled and talked.

Once the festivities got going, everyone took their seats, and the show began. Watching this on television couldn't compare to the long program while you sat in the seats. Brandon's first single from the new album received Song of the Year, and the video, which they'd filmed on their ranch, won Video of the Year, but the big prize still hung in the balance. Emma wanted him to win Entertainer of the Year. It meant everything to him, and now the moment had come. The names were read, the cameras focused on each artist's face, and the presenters arrived at the podium. Emma thought she'd be sick from the nervous butterflies in her stomach. She glanced at Beau, and his warm smile and reassuring presence calmed her jittery nerves. The presenters cut up and laughed, making jokes and dragging out the moment until she wanted to scream for them to hurry up.

When the moment came, they said, "And this year's Entertainer of the Year goes to…Brandon Tucker!" The crowd erupted in ear-shattering screams, claps, and whistles. Brandon leaned over and kissed Emma on the lips before making his way to the stage in front of his peers and fans.

With his award held aloft, he said, "Thank you so much for this. You have no idea how much it means to me to the have the respect and love of all my fans and family." He stopped for a moment like he needed gather himself, and Emma wanted to hug him. This past year of touring had taken its toll on him, her, and Beau, but they'd made it.

Beau took her hand and squeezed her fingers between his. "He'll be fine. Give him a minute."

"Sorry folks," he choked out as a tear escaped and slid down his cheek. He brushed it away with his fingers and motioned for her and Beau to come up to the stage.

"What's he doin'?"

"I don't know, darlin'," Beau replied, taking her hand and helping her waddle up the stage stairs.

Being seven months pregnant with their first child made it hard for her to get around these days, but she wouldn't have missed tonight for anything. Tonight belonged to Brandon. He'd spent months and months traveling back and forth from shows while she and Beau kept the home fires burning. Beau had stayed home with her, holding her every night, working the cattle they had, breaking horses, raising the bulls Beau wanted, and being ranch owners, while Brandon toured. Sometimes she and Beau flew to where he was playing so they could spend some time together as a trio, but it had been hard on Brandon. When she'd realized she would be having their child, she hadn't been able to hold back. She'd told Beau first, since Brandon was doing a show in San Antonio that night. Beau took matters into his own hands and flew them both out to be with Brandon when she told him about the coming birth of their child. They'd laughed, cried, kissed, and made love while they'd wrapped her in their loving arms.

"Brandon?" she asked when they made it to his side.

"Hush, wife," he scolded and a twittering of laughter echoed through the hall. "I'm sorry to take so long, but I need to say this in front of everyone. This award goes to all three of us. Emma has been my rock over the last year and a half, and Beau—God, Beau. You've been one of the most important people in my life since I started this crazy circus ride."

The crowd laughed again.

"We all know being a country music artist isn't all fun, games, and money. It's hard work. You're gone for days, weeks, or months at a time while your family stays home and keeps things normal. Beau and Emma have been keeping my life stable for the last eighteen months while I pursued my dream of being a singer. Today, with my wife," he moved his hand over her protruding belly, "my child, and my twin brother by my side, I thank you from the bottom of my heart for this award." He held the award up with one hand and wrapped his arm around her waist. "Here's to all of you, my fans. The best is yet to come!"

The End

About The Author

Sandy Sullivan is a romance author, who, when not writing, spends her time with her husband Shaun on their farm in middle Tennessee. She loves to ride her horses, play with their dogs and relax on the porch, enjoying the rolling hills of her home south of Nashville. Country music is a passion of hers and she loves to listen to it while she writes, although when she writes sex scenes, it has to be completely quiet.

She is an avid reader of romance novels and enjoys reading Nora Roberts, Jude Deveraux and Susan Wiggs. Finding new authors and delving into something different helps feed the need for literature. A registered nurse by education, she loves to help people and spread the enjoyment of romance to those around her with her novels. She loves cowboys so you'll find many of her novels have sexy men in tight jeans and cowboy boots.

www.romancestorytime.com

Other Books by Sandy Sullivan

Love Me Once, Love Me Twice (Montana Cowboys 1)

Gotta Love A Cowboy (Want Ads 1)

Before The Night Is Over (Montana Cowboys 2)

Country Minded Cougar (Hot Flash)

Secret Cravings Publishing

www.secretcravingspublishing.com

Made in the USA
Charleston, SC
12 February 2013